Lacey saw a blur of movement from a figure racing out onto the path. He was masked, featureless. Terrifying.

Lacey screamed, then felt something slam into her. Jude. He was shoving her back the way they'd come, shouting for her to run.

She ran several yards back up the path, her heart beating so hard and so loud that she could hear nothing else. Not her panting breath. Not her feet slamming against the ground. Not Jude running beside her.

Jude.

She skidded to a stop, turning to see him on the ground, struggling with their attacker.

She couldn't leave him there to fight alone.

She raced back, fishing in her pocket and pulling out her cell phone. She dialed quickly, shouting their location to the 911 operator.

Something flashed in the sunlight that filtered through the trees. A knife.

Lacey's heart nearly stopped as she lunged forward and grabbed the blade plunging toward Jude's throat.

Books by Shirlee McCoy

Love Inspired Suspense   Steeple Hill Trade

Die Before Nightfall   *Still Waters*
Even in the Darkness
When Silence Falls
Little Girl Lost
Valley of Shadows
Stranger in the Shadows
Missing Persons
Lakeview Protector
*The Guardian's Mission
*The Protector's Promise
Cold Case Murder
*The Defender's Duty

*The Sinclair Brothers

SHIRLEE McCOY

has always loved making up stories. As a child, she daydreamed elaborate tales in which she was the heroine—gutsy, strong and invincible. Though she soon grew out of her superhero fantasies, her love for storytelling never diminished. She knew early that she wanted to write inspirational fiction, and began writing her first novel when she was a teenager. Still, it wasn't until her third son was born that she truly began pursuing her dream of being published. Three years later she sold her first book. Now a busy mother of four, Shirlee is a homeschool mom by day and an inspirational author by night. She and her husband and children live in Washington and share their house with a dog, two cats and a bird. You can visit her Web site at www.shirleemccoy.com, or e-mail her at shirlee@shirleemccoy.com.

The
DEFENDER'S DUTY

Shirlee McCoy

Steeple Hill®

Published by Steeple Hill Books™

STEEPLE HILL BOOKS

Steeple
Hill®

ISBN-13: 978-0-373-44337-6
ISBN-10:   0-373-44337-4

THE DEFENDER'S DUTY

www.SteepleHill.com

Printed in U.S.A.

Forget the former things; do not dwell on the past.
See, I am doing a new thing!
Now it springs up; do you not perceive it?
I am making a way in the desert
and streams in the wasteland.
—Isaiah 43:18–19

To my family: Rodney, Jude, Caleb, Seth, Emma Grace and the daughter I have yet to meet. Ed and Shirley. Mary Ellen, Eldridge, Skylar and Trey. Beth, Rob, Joshua, Danielle, Kaitlyn and Jeremiah. Jonathan, Valerie, Jake, John, Elijah, Evelyn Grace and my nephew who hasn't made his appearance. Sara, Nate, Kai and Noah. Kitty. Melissa. Lynde, Brianna, Elijah, Amirah and Olivia. I am so blessed to have you all in my life!

And a special thanks to Elizabeth Mazer who has worked through the three Sinclair brothers books with me and whose keen eye has made each story better. In the words of my thirteen-year-old son— you rock!

ONE

The person breaking into Jude Sinclair's house wasn't being quiet about it. That suited Jude just fine. He might not be able to move as quickly as he used to, but his NYPD service weapon was in his hand, lightweight, and deadly. An old friend. A comforting one. As far as Jude was concerned that more than evened the odds.

He pressed close to the living-room wall, his view of the front door unobstructed, his heart beating slow and steady as he waited in the darkness. Anticipated. Even prayed. Let it be the guy who'd run him down. The one who had ended his career, taken the life he'd had in New York. Who had stalked him for the past two months, waiting for an opportunity to finish what he'd started—murder.

The doorknob rattled, and a soft thud carried through the thick wood. Jude frowned. The guy might have murder on his mind, but he seemed to be having trouble following through on it. Come on. How hard was it to break into a house?

Pain shot up Jude's left leg, and he shifted his weight, irritated by his weakness but refusing to be distracted by it. Just another minute and he'd finally be able to put a face to the person who'd almost killed him. He wouldn't let anything get in the way of that. Not pain or impatience or any of the hot emotions that swelled up and threatened to spill out as he waited.

One minute.

Two.

The doorknob rattled again, the lock slid open and the door creaked. Cold, crisp air blew into the house, filling the darkness with the scent of spring rain and flowers. Definitely not something he should be smelling in the winter. Jude frowned, his hand tightening on the gun as a shadow moved into the foyer. Short. Maybe five foot two.

A woman?

Or a very short man.

The light went on, and Jude lifted the gun, aiming it at the head of a very young, very scrawny woman. Pale-blond hair, creamy skin, delicate features.

A murderer?

Maybe, but she looked like a fairy-tale princess come to life. The kind that danced around forests with singing animals, completely oblivious to danger. The fact that she was humming under her breath and tapping a beat against her thigh while he pointed a gun in her direction only added to the impression.

Could she have cold-bloodedly run him down when he'd stopped to help a stranded motorist two months ago?

Jude wasn't sure, but he was about to find out. "Next time you decide to break into someone's house, you might want to be quieter about it."

She screamed, her eyes going wide and dark with terror as she finally caught sight of Jude. She screamed again when she noticed the gun, jumping back and nearly tumbling out the front door.

Jude raced after her, his left leg howling a protest, his right throbbing with pain. He grimaced, but kept running. Recovering from almost losing his legs stunk. Actually losing them would have been a whole lot worse, so he figured he couldn't complain. He also figured he wasn't going to let the blond-haired woman get away before he found out why she'd broken into his house.

She was fast, but even with pins and rods in both legs, Jude was faster. He snagged the back of her coat as she pulled open the door of a beat-up Mustang convertible.

"Let me go." She rounded on him, slamming her open palm toward his nose.

He just missed getting a face full of pain, and that irritated him. It used to be he could take down a three-hundred-pound man with ease. Now he was barely managing to restrain a hundred-pound woman.

He grabbed the woman's arm, tugging it behind her back but not exerting pressure. He didn't want to hurt her. He wanted answers. "Sorry, lady. You can't go anywhere until you tell me why you were in my house tonight."

"Your house? But…" Her voice trailed off, and she glanced over her shoulder, frowning. "You're Jude Sinclair."

"Were you expecting someone else?" He kept his grip light as he urged the woman back to the house.

"I wasn't expecting anyone. I must have mixed up the house numbers somehow. I'm sure the key had my name on it." She seemed to be talking to herself and used her free arm to reach into her coat pocket. To get keys? Or something a lot more deadly?

Jude pressed his gun lightly into her back. "Don't."

She froze. "I heard you were difficult, but nobody told me you were crazy."

"Not crazy. Cautious. Who are you?"

"Lacey Carmichael."

"That's your name. I want to know who you are." He nudged her up the porch stairs, past a suitcase he hadn't noticed when he'd run out the door.

A suitcase?

Was the woman planning to kill him and then move in?

"I'm a home-care aide. Your brother hired me—"

"My brother?" He stopped in the brightly lit foyer, lowering his gun and letting the woman turn to face him.

Her features were delicate, her jaw sharply angled, but it was her eyes that held Jude's attention. Deep-green and flecked with brown and gold, they begged a second look and a third.

He scowled.

The woman could be plotting his death, and he was gazing into her eyes?

Smart. Really smart.

"Grayson Sinclair. He contacted my employer. Helping Hands, Incorporated. They provide full-time caregivers to people who are recovering from trauma or illness. The company was founded twenty years ago by—"

"No need to give me an oral report on the company's history. Just tell me how you ended up in my house tonight."

"My company sent me keys to both sides of the duplex when I signed the contract. I'm sure they said I was going to be staying in two-fourteen. Let me just get the case file out of my suitcase and take a look." She tried to scoot past Jude, but he shifted so that he was blocking her exit.

"Have a seat in the living room. I'm going to call my brother and see if your story checks out."

"You mean he didn't tell you I was coming?" She cocked her head to the side, studying him, her gaze touching the scar on his temple and dropping to his bare feet before moving up to his face again.

"No. He didn't. My brother knows how I feel about having another home-care aide." But that wouldn't have stopped Grayson from hiring one. When they were kids, Grayson had always thought he knew best. Time hadn't changed things.

"He told me you wouldn't be happy. He just didn't tell me you wouldn't know." She smiled, a dimple in her cheek there and gone so fast Jude almost missed it.

He ground his teeth and raked a hand over his hair, acknowledging a truth that didn't make him happy—Lacey Carmichael wasn't the one who'd attacked him, which meant that he was right back where he'd been before she'd walked through his door. Empty-handed and waiting while his would-be murderer walked free. "Now that you know, you can grab your suitcase and head out. Thanks for coming. I'm sure my brother will compensate you for your time."

"I thought you wanted to call Grayson and check on my story?"

"I'll do it after you're gone."

"Great." She moved to the door. "It's been a long drive. I guess I'll head next door and be over first thing in the morning to work out the details of our business relationship."

He grabbed her arm before she could slide past. "I don't think so, lady. You're going to get your suitcase, get back in your car and go home."

"This *is* home for the next thirty days. I'm staying in the rental unit next door while I help you recuperate from your accident. It's in the contract." She flashed her dimple again.

"And I guess that was Grayson's idea, too."

"He wanted to sweeten the pot. Helping Hands wasn't eager to send someone out here, seeing as how you've been through four home-care aides in the past six weeks."

"Five if I count you."

"You can't. I'm still here."

"Not for long. Stay put for now. I'm going to see what my brother has to say for himself." Jude limped into the kitchen, irritated with his brother, with the woman in his living room, but mostly with himself.

He lifted the phone, punching in his brother's number, his

throbbing legs making him more aggravated by the minute. He'd been hoping and praying he would finally have a chance to confront his attacker face-to-face. Instead, he was dealing with another of Grayson's attempts to take charge. Not to mention the pretty young woman who'd just walked into his life.

How old was Lacey, anyway? Seventeen or eighteen? It wouldn't surprise him to find out she was still in high school. Way too young to be wandering around by herself in the wee hours of the morning.

"You'd better have a good reason for calling me at two in the morning." Grayson's harsh greeting pulled Jude away from thoughts of Lacey Carmichael and back where they should have been—on his brother's frustrating need to stick his nose in Jude's life.

"I do. She's about five-two and a hundred pounds."

"A hundred and three." Lacey had the nerve to walk into his kitchen and butt into the conversation, her cheerful announcement doing nothing to ease Jude's irritation.

He turned to face her, ready to let her know exactly how he felt about the intrusion, but she'd grabbed the coffee grounds he'd left out on the counter and was starting a fresh pot, so he decided it wouldn't do any harm to let her finish.

"You've got woman trouble and you want to talk to me about it? That's a first." Grayson still sounded annoyed, but Jude didn't miss the hint of amusement in his voice.

"I've got another home-care aide standing in my kitchen. She says you had something to do with that."

"She's there now? She wasn't supposed to arrive until tomorrow night. I figured I'd ring you in the morning to let you know she was coming."

Jude tensed at the words, and he studied Lacey more carefully. Arriving a day early was suspicious enough. Add in the way she'd shown up in the middle of the night and gone to *his* door instead of her own... She didn't look like a threat, but that didn't mean she wasn't one. "What's her name?"

"The home-care aide?"

"Who else?"

"Lacey Carmichael."

That matched. "And her description?"

"I've never met her in person. I interviewed her over the phone. Why? What's going on?"

"I'm just wondering why a professional would show up for a job a day early." His fingers tightened on the gun, and he half expected Lacey to turn, a weapon in her hand. If she even was Lacey Carmichael.

"Because she decided to drive straight through instead of staying in a hotel. Why waste money when there was an empty house waiting for me?" She cut in again, digging through the cupboards until she found two mugs. She filled one and held it out to him, meeting his stare squarely.

He took it, looking into her eyes, looking for a lie, and finding himself caught again in their deep-green depth. If she was lying, she was good at it. Better than some hardened criminals Jude had met.

"Jude? You still there?" Grayson pulled Jude's attention back where it needed to be.

"Yeah. And I'm still teed off. I told you no more home-care aides after the last one left. I don't need one."

"Tell that to the dirty laundry piled up on your bedroom floor and the dishes that are stacked ten high in your sink."

"There's nothing on my bedroom floor." Except a layer or two of dust. Hardwood tended to collect it, and Jude hadn't gotten around to dry mopping. He would, though. Eventually. And eventually he'd also tackle the dishes and the pile of laundry sitting near the washing machine. Right now, though, his focus was on more important things. Like finding his attacker. And making sure no one else was in the line of fire when the final confrontation came. Especially not a little blond princess with fearless green eyes.

"Doesn't matter whether there is stuff on your floors or not. I hired the home-care aide. I signed the contract three days ago."

"That wasn't your decision to make, as I told you the last four times you hired home-care aides." Jude ground the words out, not even trying to rein in his anger.

"I didn't make it. The family did."

"As in you and Tristan?"

"No. As in the family. We all talked about it, and we all decided it was for the best."

"You're all wrong."

"I don't think so. You haven't been the same since your accident. We think having 'round-the-clock help will get you back to your old self more quickly. Come on, Jude. This isn't something new. We've been over it before."

"And I've told you every time that I don't need help around the house."

"Tell that to Mom and Piper. They've been cooking your meals and cleaning your house once or twice a week for almost a month."

"I didn't ask them to." Jude sounded like a spoiled kid and knew it. He took a deep breath, pushing aside his frustration. Nearly dying had taught him what was important. His family. He wouldn't risk them, couldn't risk them being hurt. "Look, Gray, I appreciate everyone's concern. I appreciate their help, but recovering is something I have to do myself."

"Why?"

"Because…" *Someone is trying to kill me, and I don't want anyone I love getting hurt because of it.* That was the reason he'd tried to keep his family at a distance since he'd arrived in Lynchburg. It was the only way he could keep them safe. But knowing Grayson, Jude was sure that bringing up that argument would only make his stubborn, overprotective brother *more* determined to help.

"Never mind. We've had this conversation before, too," Grayson growled, and Jude could picture his brother pacing the floor of his house, scowling.

"Look, Grayson—"

"You look, Jude. You pretty much cut the family out of your life for years because you wanted to prove you could go it alone. You proved it, but you also put a distance between us that I don't like and never wanted. I'd hoped that having you close by would give us a chance to be friends again."

"We've always been friends."

"Friends are people you let into your life. That's not something you've done with anyone in the family for a long time." Grayson spoke without heat, but the words were a direct blow to the heart, and Jude stalked outside, away from Lacey's curious gaze. Cold pavement numbed the soles of his feet. Too bad it wasn't cold enough to do the same to the insistent ache in his legs or the throbbing guilt in his stomach. He wanted his family far away when the killer struck again, but he didn't want to hurt them anymore than he already had. "If that's the way everyone feels, I owe you all an apology."

"What you owe us is a promise that you'll take care of yourself. We love you, Jude. And we're worried."

"Don't be. I'm fine."

"I think I've heard that a hundred times these past few weeks. I haven't believed it once." Gray sighed, and Jude's guilt multiplied. He'd moved to New York to sever the bonds that had held him so tightly to his family. He'd needed space, time to be himself, a place where he could live life without his parents and siblings watching him. Judging him. He'd found it, but he'd lost something in the process. He hadn't realized just how much until he'd come to Lynchburg and been enfolded in his family's embrace once again. It made it hurt all the more to have to keep them at a distance.

"You don't need to worry about me, Gray."

"Yeah. I do. I'm your older brother. It's my job."

"So worry, but let me take care of myself."

"How about we talk about this when the sun is up?" Typical Grayson. Changing the subject rather than conceding. At the moment, Jude had too many other things to worry about. He'd set boundaries for his brother after he figured out who was trying to kill him.

"Fine. Name your time."

"Sunday after church. Honor and I have some news. That will be as good a time as any to share it. How about we come over your place?"

"Sure." Grayson's news could only be one thing. He and Honor must be engaged. Good news for Grayson and the woman he'd fallen in love with. Great news for Jude. With wedding plans in the works, Grayson would have something to focus on besides getting Jude's life in order.

"And keep the home-care aide. At least until then, okay?"

"Maybe." Jude hung up before he and his brother could go another round. Better to save the argument until after Jude had gotten rid of Lacey. Once she was gone, there wouldn't be much Grayson could do about it. And maybe this time he'd get the hint and not hire another aide.

"Did you get everything straightened out?" Lacey stepped outside.

"Depends on what you mean by everything."

"Did your brother verify who I am?"

"Yes."

"Good. The sooner I get unpacked and settled in for the night, the happier I'll be."

"Just because he verified who you were doesn't mean you're staying."

"Actually, it does." She smiled sweetly, but Jude had a feeling there was steel beneath her charming facade.

"Look, lady—"

"Lacey. Your brother signed a contract. I don't think he plans to break it. So, for the next month, whether you like it or not, I'm going to be hanging around and helping out." For someone who looked so young, she had a strong sense of self and a degree of confidence that usually came with time and experience. Still, he doubted she'd be any more difficult to get rid of than the other four aides had been.

"That's up for debate."

"How about we talk about it in the morning?"

"How about we have some more coffee and talk about it now?" He walked into the house, knowing Lacey was following. He needed to lay things on the line for her, let her know that she wasn't staying, and then he'd say goodbye and watch Lacey Carmichael walk out of his life. Because the last thing he needed was one more complication, and it seemed to Jude that was exactly what Lacey was going to be.

TWO

Adrenaline still thrummed through Lacey's veins as she followed her new client inside. After sixteen hours of driving, she'd thought she'd slip into the duplex she'd be staying in for the next month, eat one of the packs of crackers she had in her suitcase and then get a few hours of sleep. She'd never imagined she'd find herself staring down the barrel of a gun.

Someone had made a mistake and given the wrong house number. Whether it was her supervisor or Grayson Sinclair, Lacey didn't know. All she knew was that it could have cost her her life.

"Before we discuss whether you're staying or going, I'd like the key to my place."

"I'll need it so I can get back in tomorrow morning. I wouldn't want to have to wake you."

"Hate to break the news to you, but it already is tomorrow morning, and you're already in my house." He held out a hand, and Lacey dropped the key into it. "Thanks. Coffee?"

"No. Thanks. I've already had a dozen cups today."

"I guess that explains your shaking hands." He smirked, his deep-gray eyes almost as unnerving as the gun he still held.

"Looking down the barrel of a gun will do that to a person."

"Sorry about that. I wasn't expecting company." He limped

across the living room and sat down, his dark hair falling across his forehead and partially concealing a scar that ran from his temple into his hairline. He'd been close to death but had survived. In that, she and Jude were alike.

"Do you always point guns at unexpected guests?"

"Only when they walk in uninvited. Grayson said you weren't supposed to arrive until tomorrow. You said you're here early because you didn't want to waste money on a hotel room."

"That's right."

"I was thinking it wouldn't be wasted money since your company is probably paying for your travel expenses, so I'm wondering why you decided to drive straight through."

Jude was a homicide detective. Lacey had learned that from the client information she'd received before she'd left Chicago. She just hadn't expected him to use his interrogation skills on her. "Are you always this suspicious?"

"Only when someone breaks into my house at two in the morning."

"It's not breaking in if that person has a key."

"Which doesn't answer my question."

"Too much coffee. There was no sense wasting money on a room I wasn't going to be able to sleep in. Even if it was Helping Hand's money." It was the only excuse she could come up with. The truth was much too complicated to tell and wasn't something she planned to share with a stranger. No matter how handsome and compelling he might be.

Handsome?

Compelling?

She was a lot more shaken than she'd thought if she was using those words to describe one of her clients.

"You've been on the road a long time. Where were you coming from?"

"Chicago."

"You were working there?"

"Yes. I had an elderly client who suffered from dementia. I've been living with her for the past eight months."

"And you left her to take the job my brother offered?"

"I never leave clients until they don't need me any more."

"People don't recover from dementia." Jude pressed for more information. Lacey didn't mind giving it. Part of building a good working relationship required sharing a few tidbits of personal information. It had taken a few years for Lacey to realize how important that was, but once she had, she'd been able to pick and choose the information she'd shared, offering just enough to make her clients feel comfortable without giving too much of herself away.

"Mrs. Simpson passed away four days ago."

"I'm sorry."

"I am, too, but she lived her life well until the end. And now I'm here for you."

"Actually, you're here for my family. Like I said before, I don't need a home-care aide."

"Are you trying to fire me?"

"I'm just stating a fact. I don't need help. You're here because it makes my brother feel like he's in control of things."

"Your brother is concerned about you."

"My brother is a typical oldest child. He thinks the world is his to command. I've spent most of my life trying to prove him wrong."

Surprised, she laughed, her tension easing. This she could handle. A client talking about his life? Piece of cake. "I take it you haven't succeeded yet."

"Not quite, but I'm still working on it."

"Good luck with that." She stifled a yawn. Despite too much coffee, exhaustion stole her energy and made her want nothing more than to lie down and sleep for a week.

"Looks like that drive really wore you out." Jude studied her face as if she were a mystery he had to solve. The thought made her uncomfortable. She didn't want to be studied, and she certainly didn't want to be solved.

"It did. I think I'll go next door and get settled in. I really am sorry for waking you."

"I wasn't sleeping." He stood, walking to the front door with her, his slightly hitched stride speaking of the injuries he'd suffered.

"Can I get anything for you before I go next door? Something to eat? Medicine?"

"Lacey, I'm a grown man. If I need any of those things, I'll get them myself."

"Not while I'm around. Your brother hired me—"

"To be a home-care aide. Yeah. I get that." He ran a hand down his jaw and shook his head. "But *you* need to get that I don't need you here. Go next door. We'll talk more about why you're not staying after we both get some sleep."

"Just so you know." Lacey stepped outside, shivering in the cold winter air. "I'm planning to stay."

"Just so you know, I'm the one who will be making that decision." Jude scowled, his eyes flashing with irritation.

"We'll see." She offered her best smile, pulled her suitcase inside the other half of the duplex and closed the door, blocking her view of Jude and his deep-gray eyes.

Her heart beat a little too fast and a little too hard, but at least her legs weren't shaking anymore. Dealing with difficult clients was something she did well, but Jude wasn't like any client she'd ever worked with before. He was younger. Better-looking.

Lacey frowned.

A client was a client. Jude was no different from any other man she'd worked with over the past few years.

She ran her hand along the foyer wall, flicking on the light as she had in Jude's house. She half expected to see a man standing in the living room pointing a gun in her direction. There wasn't one. Just a sofa and a chair, both in decent shape. A coffee table and an end table. A fireplace.

It was a cozy room and perfect for Lacey. She hummed as she walked down a short hallway and into a roomy kitchen, filling the silence and distracting herself from the fear that hadn't quite let her go. It was a remnant of a past she preferred to forget. After all, what was in the past couldn't hurt her anymore. All it could do was teach her how to live her life today.

The kitchen appliances were dated but serviceable, the floor faded linoleum. A sliding glass door led out into the backyard. Lacey opened it, stepping outside and shivering in the cold. A full moon peeked over the treetops, casting green light onto the overgrown backyard. Aside from the wind, nothing moved. The silent stillness seemed heavy and oppressive. Unnatural.

Lacey cocked her head, listening. Waiting. When she'd been a kid, she'd learned how to do both. Then it had been a matter of survival. Now it was simply a matter of curiosity. Something unsettling was in the air. She wasn't sure what it was, but she couldn't ignore it. She glanced around the dark yard. It was small and hid nothing from view.

A few straggly plants butted up against a tall fence. A white bench stood close to the house and two gates offered entrances and exits to the yard, one at the back of the property, the other on the side of the fence that separated Lacey's yard from Jude's. There was nothing else. She stepped back and closed the door, locking it and pulling the bolt. Whatever she'd felt, it was outside, not in the cozy house she was going to be living in for the next month.

Her own place.

It had been a long time since she'd had that. There'd been a few times over the past ten years when she'd rented an apartment, but most of her assignments came with free board. That usually meant living in the spare room in a crowded apartment or cluttered house. Having a two-bedroom, one-and-a-half-bath duplex to herself was sheer luxury. Lacey planned to enjoy it.

The thought made her smile, but it didn't chase away her unease. Maybe the long ride and lack of sleep had gotten to her. Or maybe seeing Jude glaring at her over the barrel of his gun had knocked her off balance. Either way, Lacey was sure she'd feel better after a few hours' sleep. First, though, she needed to eat.

She searched through her suitcase, sure that she had a few packages of crackers there. When she didn't find them, she went to the front door, hesitating for a moment before she opened it. Outside, the heaviness of the air had lifted and the silence seemed more natural. Still, she wasn't sure she wanted to step across the threshold and walk outside.

Then again, she wasn't sure she wanted to spend the next few hours hungry.

Her Mustang was parked a few feet from the porch and it would only take seconds to grab the duffel bag she'd left in the passenger's seat. She knew she had pretzels and a Coke in there. Her stomach rumbled, cementing her decision.

She hurried down the porch stairs and opened the car door, grabbing the duffel and locking the car again. "We wouldn't want someone to steal you, Bess. Another hundred thousand miles and you'll officially be a relic. Don't worry, I won't get rid of you. I'll just get you a nip and a tuck and a brand-new engine."

"Do you always talk to your car?" The voice was as deep and rich as dark chocolate, and Lacey recognized it immediately.

She pivoted, searching the shadows until she caught sight of Jude's tall, rangy form near the corner of the house. His shoulder was pressed against the siding as if he needed the support to stay on his feet.

That concerned Lacey, and she walked to his side, studying his face in the moon's reflected light. "Bess isn't a car. She's a personality."

"She looks it. How long have you had her?"

"I bought her when I was a senior in high school."

"So, that was what? Five years ago?"

"I'm flattered, but high school was a few more years ago than that."

"Seven, then. Or eight."

"Try eleven."

"That makes you, what? Twenty-nine?"

"Twenty-eight. Soon to be twenty-nine. Not that I'm counting or anything." She smiled, wishing she could see his face more clearly.

Why was he outside leaning against the house instead of inside sleeping?

If she'd known him better, she would have asked. Lots of her clients suffered from insomnia. Some because of pain. Others because they knew the end was near and didn't want to miss a minute of time. She had a feeling something else had Jude up wandering around outside in the wee hours of the morning.

"Why wouldn't you want to count? You're still a babe in the woods."

"Not even close." She unzipped the duffel and pulled out the bag of pretzels, opening it quickly and eating one. What she really wanted was chocolate. Lots of it. Based on what she'd seen so far, working for Jude was going to be a three-chocolate-bar-a-day job. She should have grabbed her emergency supply from the glove compartment, but there was no way she was going to do it now. Not while Jude was watching with dark, curious eyes.

"Hungry?"

"Starving."

"Let me guess. You didn't want to waste money stopping to eat on your way here."

"Something like that." And she hadn't wanted to stop until she'd reached the assignment. She liked being busy. Downtime wasn't something she handled well. Fortunately, Helping Hands had plenty of business, and Lacey never had more than a day or two when she wasn't working.

"Then I wouldn't want to keep you from your early-morning snack. Enjoy it." He straightened and limped toward the back of the house, dismissing Lacey with an abruptness that other people might have found rude.

Lacey found it telling.

Pain often made people want to hide away from the world. According to his client file, Jude had been living with intense pain for two months. Who knew what was on his mind or in his heart because of it?

She fell into step beside him.

"Pretzel?" She held out the bag, but Jude ignored it.

"Go inside, Lacey. I didn't need you an hour ago, and I don't need you now."

"Who said anything about need? You're awake. I'm awake. Why not spend some time getting to know each other?"

"I'm not in the mood for company."

"That doesn't mean you don't need some."

"You're persistent. I'll give you that much." He smiled, the grim turn of his lips doing nothing to ease the harsh lines and angles of his face.

"That's why I'm good at what I do."

"I'm sure that's what the other four aides my brother hired thought. They lasted a total of two and a half weeks."

"You sound proud of that."

"Do I?" He turned and headed back to the house, the long-sleeved T-shirt he wore not nearly enough protection against the cold. At least he'd put on shoes when he'd come outside this time.

"I've worked with a lot tougher clients than you, Jude."

"You sound proud of that."

Lacey laughed, surprised that the grim-faced man beside her had any humor in him at all. "We're all good at something. I'm good at dealing with people like you."

"Like me?"

"Difficult people. People no one else wants to work with."

"I think I'm insulted."

"Why? You created your reputation."

"True, but I didn't expect you to tell me what it was to my face."

"Just because I look like a pushover doesn't mean I am one. As a matter of fact—"

"Shh." He put a hand on her shoulder, holding her in place.

"What—"

"I hear a car."

"There are lots of them around."

"Not on this road." He pulled her to a shadowy corner outside the house. "Don't move. Okay?"

She nodded, fear pulsing sharply in her chest.

Who did Jude think was coming?

The car rolled into view, turning onto the long driveway that led to the house and stopped. Dark and sleek. Newer. If there was a license plate, Lacey couldn't see it. She leaned forward, craning her neck to get a better look, but Jude tugged her back, pressing her against the house with his body. Moving into her space. Stealing her breath as he whispered in her ear. "I said don't move."

Lacey wanted to slip away, peer around the side of the house and figure out exactly what was going on, but Jude's chest pressed against her back, his breath tickling her ear, and she knew if she moved he'd only press closer. She didn't like people in her space. Especially if those people were men.

"I can't see a license plate. Stay here. I'm going to see if I can get a look at the driver." Jude eased away, and Lacey breathed a sigh of relief, turning to face him.

"You can't—" The words lodged in her throat as she caught sight of Jude's gun.

"Sure I can. Stay here, Lacey. I don't want to shoot the wrong person."

"Jude!"

But he'd already moved away, was slipping through the darkness, part of the shadows and barely visible.

Leaving her standing in the darkness. Alone. Praying that whoever was in that car had a good reason for idling at the top of the driveway and that Jude wouldn't end up killing someone. Or being killed.

Having her client murdered while she watched was not how Lacey intended to spend her first night in Lynchburg. She pulled her cell phone from her pocket, frowning when she realized the battery had died.

Stupid, Lacey.

Don't you ever think?

The words were from the past, and she pushed them aside. She couldn't use her cell phone, but she could keep her new client from getting himself killed.

She hoped.

"A plan would be nice right about now, Lord." She whispered the prayer as she crept toward the front of the house. Her door was unlocked and open. All she had to do was get inside and call the police.

Piece of cake.

Sure it was.

The car rolled closer to the house. Jude inched closer to the car. And Lacey tiptoed toward the front door. All of them pawns in a macabre chess game.

It was a shame Lacey had never been very good at chess.

She kept moving anyway, danger breathing down her neck, reminding her of other nights, other dark, shadowy places. Terror. Anger. The overwhelming need to survive.

Memories better left in the darkest recesses of her mind.

Gravel crunched. Jude whispered something into the night. And Lacey was pulled firmly back into the present and the menace that seemed to fill the air and deepen the darkness, stealing the light and threatening to steal everything Lacey had worked so hard for.

THREE

Jude knew he'd told Lacey to stay put. Twice. Yet there she was, creeping toward her front door, just begging to be shot by whoever was driving the black Honda sedan. "Get down."

He whispered the command for the second time, but she kept on going. He had no choice but to change his course and follow. He'd spent enough years working as a beat cop in New York City to sense danger. Right now it was nipping at his heels just as it had been in the weeks preceding the accident that had almost taken his life.

Accident.

That's what his supervisor insisted it was. That's what the police report indicated. It's not what Jude believed. Someone had tried to kill him two months ago, accelerating toward him as he helped a stranded motorist. There wasn't a doubt in Jude's mind that the act had been deliberate. Nor did he doubt that the person would try again.

But next time, Jude would be ready.

The car inched forward, moving as quietly as a car could. Nearly coasting. Lights off. License plate concealed. And instead of moving toward it, Jude was heading up the porch stairs, his need to keep Lacey safe outweighing his need to confront the driver of the car.

It was the same need to protect that had nearly gotten him killed. He'd been on vacation, heading out to a cabin in upstate New York when he'd spotted a woman and two kids standing on the side of the road, steam rising from the hood of their minivan.

He could have passed them like everyone else had, but denying someone help wasn't something Jude had ever been able to do. He'd pulled up behind the car, gotten out of his vehicle and been run down by a black sedan.

One that looked a lot like the one idling at the end of his driveway.

"Get away from the door. You're lit up like a Christmas tree." He hissed the warning as he tugged her out of the light from the door and into the shadowy corner of the porch.

"What's going on, Jude? Who's in the car?"

"I'll let you know as soon as I find out. Stay here."

"But—"

"We'll talk after I deal with my visitor."

He limped down the porch steps and jogged toward the car, his gun in hand, knowing he and Lacey had already been seen. Maybe, if he were lucky, he'd get a glimpse of the driver anyway. And maybe he wouldn't get a bullet through the heart while he did it.

The car U-turned, kicking up gravel as it sped away.

Gone.

A missed opportunity.

And Jude knew exactly who to blame.

He gritted his teeth and made his way back up the stairs, slamming his fist on Lacey's door as he moved into the foyer.

"There's no need to slam things around." Lacey stepped inside and closed the door, her shoulders stiff. Jude wasn't sure if she was scared or angry, and he wasn't sure he cared.

"Sure there is. I've been waiting months to confront the person in that car. Thanks to you, it didn't happen."

"Thanks to me? I was trying to save your sorry hide."

"I didn't need saving. I needed to get a good look at the car's driver." He stalked away before he could say anything worse. Lacey didn't know what was going on, and she couldn't be blamed for not understanding.

"I'm sorry, Jude. I just wanted to help." She touched his arm, her fingers warm through his shirt, searing his skin and cooling his temper.

"There are things going on that you don't understand, Lacey. For now on, when I tell you to do something, do it."

He limped back outside, his legs protesting every step, and watched as the retreating car braked at the top of the road. Two months ago, Jude would have sprinted around the side of the house, hopped into his car and sped after the retreating vehicle. Unfortunately, his sprinting days were over.

That didn't mean he wouldn't try to find the car and its driver.

"I'm going for a drive. You go back in the house, eat your pretzels and then try to get some sleep," he called over his shoulder as he started down the porch steps.

"There you go again. Trying to order me around." Lacey shut the front door and hurried after him.

"I'm not trying. I'm doing it."

"And wasting time while you're at it. I don't know who you think is in that car, but if you're planning to catch up to him, the sooner we follow, the better."

"*We're* not following. *I* am."

"My car is right in front of the house, and I've got the key."

She didn't add that it would make more sense to take her car since it was obviously closer than his. Probably because she knew she didn't have to. Jude hadn't made the grade as a homicide detective because he was ruled by his emotions. He'd made it because he was logical and meticulous.

"Fine," he said. "We'll take your car."

"I knew you'd be reasonable."

"I knew you'd be annoying."

She laughed, the sound ringing through the night, nudging at Jude's soul, telling him he needed to lighten up a little, stop taking things so seriously.

Unfortunately, that was hard to do with a killer stalking him.

He walked to Lacey's car, his limping stride only adding to his frustration. Since the accident, his body no longer felt like his own. His legs were foreign and difficult to move. His back was stiff. Every day was filled with challenges, but what bugged Jude the most was that he couldn't take off after the bad guys, chase the villains, bring them in and see justice served.

"You're awfully quiet. You're not feeling sorry for yourself, are you?" Lacey opened the car door and slid into the driver's seat, clearly not caring that Jude was seething with frustration.

"Isn't that your job?" He shut her door and got in the passenger's seat.

"To feel sorry for you? Why would I? You've got a nice home, a family that loves you. What's there to be sorry about?"

"Two bum legs and a lost career." He muttered the response, but knew she was right. He had plenty to be thankful for and not much to be sorry about. Even less once he figured out who was trying to kill him.

"I've met a lot of people who thrived with more hardship than that." She put on her seat belt, adjusted the mirrors, glanced over her shoulder and fiddled with the dashboard buttons until Jude grabbed the key from her hand and shoved it into the ignition. "There. We're ready."

"Right." She gripped the wheel with both hands and drove backward down the driveway and onto the road. The speedometer crept from five to fifteen miles an hour and hovered there until Jude wanted to wrench the steering wheel out from under Lacey's hands and stomp down hard on the gas pedal.

"I suppose there's a reason why you're driving so slow?"

"Slow? The speed limit is posted. Fifteen miles an hour."

"Fifteen miles an hour if you're not trying to catch a potential murderer." Although at this point, it was unlikely they'd come within twenty miles of the guy who'd been behind the wheel of the car they were trying to follow.

"Murderer? You actually think the guy was here to…" Apparently she couldn't get the words out, but Jude had no problem with them.

"Kill me."

"What?" She braked hard, pulled to the side of the road and turned to face Jude. "Grayson said you were troubled, but he didn't say you were paranoid."

"I'm not." He knew that wouldn't be enough information to get Lacey driving again, but wasting time chit-chatting wasn't high on his list of things to do when a criminal was escaping.

"You know you can't tell me someone is trying to kill you and expect me to act as though this is just an ordinary early-morning outing, right?"

"You knew it wasn't an ordinary outing when you offered to drive, and what I expect you to do is drive."

To Jude's surprise, she accelerated, pulling onto the road and heading in the direction the sedan had gone. The street was dark, the houses that lined it silent and sleeping. There were plenty of cars parked in driveways and on the side of the road, and Jude scanned each as Lacey drove past. He didn't expect to find his quarry, but he hoped. That would have to be enough for now.

"If we see the car, we're going to call the police, right? Let them deal with it." Lacey's question filled the silence, reminding Jude that he wasn't alone in his quest. There was someone else to think about; someone who could easily be hurt.

"If we see the car, you'll call the police and wait in here until they arrive." No way would Jude allow Lacey anywhere near the vehicle.

"What about you?"

"I'll do what I have to do to make sure the person doesn't drive away before the police arrive." He scanned the street as he spoke, his hope of finding the car dying a little more with each passing minute. He wanted to find it, prayed he'd find it, but he doubted either would do any good. After all, he'd wanted to walk out of the hospital on two strong, pain-free legs. Instead, he'd been rolled out in a wheelchair. As for praying, Jude had walked too far away from his faith to expect God to answer.

It had only been recently that he'd realized how true that was. Being forced to slow down had given him time to take a long, hard look at his life. He wasn't sure he liked what he saw. He'd spent eleven years working hard, playing hard, pursuing his passions with the same single-minded zeal with which he'd pursued criminals.

He wanted to believe there was nothing wrong with that, but a quiet voice in his soul kept whispering that he'd taken the wrong path. That his need for independence had cost him the things he'd valued most—faith and family.

He didn't have time to dwell on it.

Someone wanted him dead. If Jude didn't find out who that was, he wouldn't have to worry about the things he'd given up to gain freedom and independence. He wouldn't have to worry about anything at all.

"We're probably not going to find the car." Lacey echoed Jude's doubts, but that didn't mean he planned to give up.

"That doesn't mean we shouldn't keep looking."

"We *could* keep looking. Or we could go back to the house."

"And do what? Hope the guy comes back?"

"Actually, I was hoping we could raid your fridge and find something for breakfast."

Lacey's answer made Jude smile. "Is food the only thing you think about?"

"Not usually, but I haven't had anything to eat in twelve hours."

"You had pretzels."

"They don't count. Or that's what I'll be telling myself when I'm gorging on pancakes, sausage, grits and home fries."

"Sorry to say, I don't have any of those things in my fridge. Not that I think you could actually eat all that."

"Point me to a restaurant that's open all night and I'll be happy to prove you wrong." She sounded serious, and Jude was sure he heard her stomach growl.

"There's an all-night diner a couple of miles down this road. We can stop there."

"Does that mean we're done looking for the guy in the black sedan?" She sounded so hopeful, Jude almost felt bad about telling her the truth.

"We'll keep looking until we get there. If we don't find him by then, we probably won't."

"Too bad."

It was, because there was no way the driver of the sedan was going to drive away for good. He'd be back, and when he returned there was no guarantee Jude would see him coming. The way Jude saw it, most people never experienced a miracle in their lives. He'd already experienced one in surviving the driver's first attack. There was no way he could count on another.

All he could do was wait and hope that when the time came, he'd be ready to fight.

FOUR

Lacey didn't believe in spending a lot of time worrying. It wasted valuable energy that was better spent enjoying other things. Unfortunately, worry was exactly what she was feeling.

Someone wanted Jude dead.

That was what he'd said, and despite initial doubts, Lacey believed him.

She'd worked with enough paranoid clients to know one when she saw one. She didn't see one when she looked at Jude. She saw instead a man on a mission. One who knew exactly what he was doing and why.

She tightened her grip on the steering wheel and stared out at the road, praying desperately that she wouldn't see the car Jude was looking for. If she did, Jude would want her to pull over so that he could confront the driver. Lacey wasn't sure she could bring herself to do it.

Sure, Jude had a gun…but who knew what the guy in the car had?

She inched down the street in good old Bess, the Mustang's loud engine masking any sounds from outside the vehicle. A parade of murderers in black sedans could have been speeding up behind her and she wouldn't have known it.

"You can relax, Lacey. We're not going to find him tonight." Jude's voice was smooth and deep, the kind that could be filled with promises or with threats and still send shivers along the spine.

"Maybe we should call the police."

"And tell them what?" He snarled the question as Lacey spotted the all-night diner and pulled into the parking lot.

"There's no need to snap."

"I'm not snapping. I'm…" He smoothed his hair and turned to face her, the planes and hollows of his face shadowed, his eyes dark. "Snapping. Sorry."

"It's okay. I guess if I thought someone wanted me dead, I'd be snapping, too."

"I already told you, I don't think it. I know it. I was nearly killed two months ago. It wasn't an accident. Unfortunately, I don't have the evidence I need to prove it."

"You were run down while you were helping a stranded motorist. I'm sure you know how often that happens. The fact that the car accelerated could mean that the person driving it was drunk. It doesn't necessarily mean he was specifically targeting you." Lacey made the argument without believing in it. Jude had worked as a homicide detective. She didn't believe he'd jump to conclusions about what had happened.

"That's what NYPD said. With no other attacks against me, they had no choice but to call the accident a hit-and-run."

"I'm sorry."

"Why?" He met her eyes, searched her face, seemed to see much more than other people did. Much more than Lacey wanted him to see.

"Because it hurts when the people you care about won't help you." She knew that more than most, but that was a part of the past she preferred not to dwell on.

"You've hit the nail on the head with that one. You said you were hungry. Let's go eat." He opened his door, cutting off further conversation.

By the time she got out of the car, Jude was already standing by her door, tapping his fingers impatiently on the roof of the car and scanning the other parked cars. "You move pretty slowly for a woman with two good legs."

"And you're awfully impatient for a guy who's got nothing better to do than stand around waiting for me."

"Who said I don't have better things to do?"

"Your brother said you're on medical leave."

"I am. That doesn't mean I'm not working." He put a hand on her lower back and urged her toward the diner, his touch firm and gentle, his stride hitched but confident.

If she hadn't been looking so closely, Lacey wouldn't have noticed the sheen of sweat that beaded his brow or the deep lines that bracketed his mouth. Pain. He was in a lot of it, but a guy like Jude would never admit it.

He held the diner's door, his mouth set in a grim line, and Lacey decided it was time to take control of the situation. She motioned a waitress over and pointed to a booth that overlooked the parking lot. It was near the door, had wide benches set close enough together that Jude could put his feet up and offered a quick escape if he was feeling too bad to stay. "Do you mind if we sit there?"

"Go ahead. You're in early, Mr. Sinclair. Or late. Guess it depends on how you look at it." The young waitress glanced from Jude to Lacey and back again, her kohl-rimmed eyes and pierced brow at odds with the sweet innocence of her face.

"We'll just call it both." Jude smiled, but to Lacey it looked more like a grimace. He needed to sit down. Not stand around chatting with the waitress.

"How about we discuss it at the table?" She took his arm, tugging him toward the booth and offering the waitress an apologetic smile. Rudeness wasn't Lacey's thing, but taking care of her clients was.

"Want me to bring you your usual, Mr. Sinclair?"

"Coffee would be good, but no pie."

"How about bread? We've got fresh pumpkin bread. I helped Louis make it an hour ago."

"Sure. Why not?" Jude dropped into the seat, wincing a little as he slid toward the window.

"How about you, ma'am? Can I get you something while you're looking at the menu?" The girl turned her full attention on Lacey. Bold pink strands of hair were woven liberally through her dark-brown locks, and her stance said she was ready for a fight. To Lacey, looking at her was like looking into the past and seeing herself as she'd been as a teenager. Alone. Scared.

Lacey blinked, surprised that she'd be thinking about that time in her life. The girl she'd been had ceased to exist so long ago it was as if she'd never been. God had given Lacey a second chance, a new life. If she kept focused on that, everything else would be okay. "Coffee would be great. Three creams. Two sugars. A slice of the pumpkin bread and a cup of whatever your soup of the day is."

"Corn chowder."

"Great." Lacey forced a smile and fished in her pocket for the packets of Tylenol she kept there. Like Jude, she'd been through her share of trauma. She still felt the effects of it years later. Right now, Jude needed the pain reliever a lot more than she did. She tore open the pack, dumping two caplets in her hand and holding them out to Jude. "Take these."

He looked at the medicine and frowned. "What are you? A walking pharmacy?"

"Just a woman who likes to be prepared."

"I appreciate the effort, but I don't need it."

"Sure you do. You just don't want to man up and admit it."

"'Man up'?" His lips quirked in a half smile that softened the hard angles of his face.

"That's what I said." She smiled back, staring into his eyes. At the moment they were velvety and warm, inviting in a way she hadn't noticed when she'd looked into them before.

Dangerous in a way she wouldn't dare acknowledge.

"All right. You win. This time." He took the caplets from her hand and swallowed them dry. "I think I could take another three and they wouldn't touch the pain."

Lacey covered his hand, squeezing it gently. "Why don't we go back home? I'm not *that* hungry, and you obviously need something stronger than a couple of Tylenol."

"Even if I were back home, I wouldn't take anything more than what you just gave me." He flipped his hand, capturing hers before she could pull it away. "So, tell me, Lacey, what convinced you to travel all the way from Chicago to work for a guy like me?"

"I haven't had my own place in a while. When I was told I would if I came to Lynchburg, I knew I couldn't pass up the opportunity." But that was only part of the reason she'd taken the job. The other reason wasn't as concrete. The feeling she'd gotten when she'd first spoken to Grayson about his brother had chased her into her dreams and refused to let her go. She had to take the job. The more she'd prayed about it, the more she'd understood the necessity of it.

"You drove halfway across the country to have your own place?"

"Exactly."

He eyed her for a moment, his eyes winter-gray and filled with questions. "I guess you want me to believe that."

"Why wouldn't you?"

"Because you don't seem very materialistic, and I have a feeling you would live in far worse conditions if it meant helping someone in need."

He was right.

And that bothered Lacey.

Jude had only met her a few hours ago and already knew more about her than most clients learned in a month. "Who says I'm not materialistic?"

"Your car." His gaze dropped to her faded sweater, but he had the good grace not to mention it.

"Bess is an icon. I'd never replace her."

"Bess is a piece of junk that needs a new engine and a paint job."

He was right. Again. "There's nothing wrong with having an old car."

"Not for someone who isn't materialistic. Which brings me back to my main point. I don't think you came here for the house."

Obviously, he was going to keep pushing until he got an answer he liked. There wasn't one, so Lacey gave him what she could. "After I talked to my supervisor and your brother, I prayed about taking the job. It felt like the right thing to do, so I did."

"You prayed about it?"

"Is there something wrong with that?"

"Not at all. I just haven't met many people who make decisions based on prayer."

"Maybe that's why so many people are making so many bad decisions."

"You've got a point there. I know I've made a few in my life. Maybe if I'd stopped to pray about them, I wouldn't have." He smiled, releasing her hand as the waitress set coffee and plates of pumpkin bread on the table.

"Soup is coming right out. You want to order now, or wait until I bring it?"

"I'd like a grilled cheese sandwich." Lacey handed the menu back to the waitress, the sleeve of her sweater riding up and revealing the pale white scars that encircled her wrist. She dropped her arm, shooting a glance in Jude's direction. He seemed occupied with the slice of bread he was devouring. Good. The last thing she wanted were more questions.

"Anything for you, Mr. Sinclair?"

"No. Thanks, Jenna."

"You sure? We've got a great chicken pot pie today."

"Another time. Thanks, though."

"Suit yourself." The young woman scribbled something on her order pad, her lips pressed tightly together. At Jenna's age, Lacey had been working the same kind of job, and she remembered the nights when she'd calculated the tips and worried about whether or not she was going to earn enough to keep the lights turned on.

"You know, I think I'll take some of that chicken pot pie."

"So you want that instead of the grilled cheese?"

"No. I'll take both. Just box the pot pie so I can take it home for tomorrow. Can you throw in a couple more slices of the pumpkin bread while you're at it?"

"All right. It'll be a few minutes. Just raise a hand if you need a refill on the coffee before then." Jenna walked away, and Lacey grabbed three creamers and dumped them into her coffee.

"You could have just left her a big tip." Jude spoke quietly.

"That would have been charity. I don't think Jenna would have appreciated it."

"Good call. I tried to slip her an extra twenty one time, and she followed me outside to tell me what I could do with it."

"She did not." But Lacey knew Jenna had. She would have done the same at that age.

"She did. She informed me that there were a lot of people who were a lot worse off than she was and that I should take the money and give it to one of them."

"Did you?"

"What do you think?"

"I think you found another way to give it to her."

"I gave it to her boss and asked that it be added to her tips. I found it taped to my front door the next day."

"Good for Jenna."

"You think? The way I see it, pride goeth before a fall. Jenna may be on her way to falling hard."

"If she does, she'll learn from it."

"You sound like you know what you're talking about."

"Everyone falls sometimes, Jude." *Some people just fall harder than others.*

"Yeah. That's something I'm learning." He grabbed a second piece of pumpkin bread, and Lacey frowned.

"Didn't your mother teach you to share?"

"She tried." He grinned, split the piece and handed her half. "Happy now?"

"I'd be happier if you'd given me the whole piece."

"Didn't *your* mother teach *you* to share?"

"My mother didn't teach me much of anything." The words slipped out before she thought them through, and Lacey wished them back immediately.

"You know that comment begs me to ask a dozen questions, right?"

"You can ask. That doesn't mean I'll answer." She met Jude's gaze, refusing to fidget beneath his scrutiny.

"Understood. So I'll go ahead and start asking. You don't get along with your mom?" he asked, as Jenna set a plate of food and a brown paper bag in front of Lacey.

"There you go," Jenna said. "I'm off shift. If you need anything else, you'll have to flag down one of the other waitresses."

"I'm sure we'll be fine." Lacey dug through her wallet, pulling out her last two twenties. "You can ring up our tab before you go."

"I'll have your change for you in a minute."

"Make it my change and keep it." Jude nudged Lacey's money aside and pressed several bills into Jenna's hand.

She thanked him and hurried away, leaving Lacey with her two twenties still waving in the breeze.

"Here." Lacey held out the money, frowning when Jude waved it away. "Take the money, Jude. I like to pay my own way."

"I'm sure you do, but we don't have time for an argument. Take a look outside. What do you see?"

She looked and shrugged. "The parking lot."

"Can you see your car?"

"Sure. It's parked under the streetlight. Why?"

"See the car to its left?"

"Yeah. It's a black sedan." Her heart skipped a beat as she said the words, and she leaned closer to the glass. "You don't think that's the same car, do you?"

"I don't know, but I'm going to find out."

Lacey scooped up the grilled cheese sandwich and shoved it into the carryout bag. "Let's go."

He eyed her for a moment, his jaw set, his gaze hot. "*We're* not going anywhere. You are staying here. I am going to talk to the driver of that car."

"I think we've been down this road before, and I'm pretty sure we both know where it leads."

"It leads to you getting fired. Stay put until I get back or forget about having a place of your own for a month." He stood and limped away, not even giving Lacey a second glance as he crossed the room and headed into the kitchen area.

Probably heading for a back door.

Lacey gave him a one-minute head start and then followed, the hair on the back of her neck standing on end and issuing a warning she couldn't ignore. Danger. It was somewhere close by again, and there was no way she was going to let Jude walk into it alone. If he fired her, so be it. As a matter of fact, if he fired her, it might be for the best. Jude wasn't the kind of client she was used to working for. Sure, there'd been other young men, but none of them had seemed quite as vital or alive as Jude. She told herself that it made her uncomfortable because he didn't seem to need her, and Lacey didn't want to be where she wasn't needed. Told herself that, but didn't quite believe it. Jude was trouble. And not just because someone was trying to kill him. On the other hand, she'd felt absolutely certain moving to Lynchburg was what God wanted her to do.

"So, which is it, Lord? Right or wrong?" She whispered the words as she slipped into the diner's hot kitchen. A cook glared at her, but she ignored him. Until she knew for sure why God had brought her to Lynchburg, Lacey could only do what she'd been paid to—make sure Jude was okay. Even if that meant putting herself in danger.

Lacey took a deep breath, prayed that whoever was in the car didn't have a weapon and pushed open the door. The area behind the diner was dark and silent, the shadow of the building hiding her as she stepped into the parking lot. There were no cars there, just empty spaces ready for the breakfast rush. The emptiness should have comforted Lacey. Instead, it reminded her of how alone she was. Maybe waiting inside the diner would have been a better idea, but Lacey wasn't good at waiting and didn't believe in leaving others to fight their battles alone. Jude was about to face his enemy. She had every intention of being with him when he did. Heart slamming in her chest, pulse racing, she hurried around the side of the building and headed toward whatever trouble waited.

FIVE

Jude eased around the corner of the restaurant, the dark alleyway offering him perfect cover as he peered into the parking lot. The car he'd spotted through the window of the restaurant was still parked beside Lacey's. Black. Four-door. Honda. It matched the one that had pulled up in front of his house and the one that had run him down in New York.

He needed to get closer.

A soft sound came from behind him. A rustle of fabric. A sigh of breath. Spring rain and wildflowers carried on the cold night air. Lacey.

Of course.

"I told you you were going to be fired if you didn't stay where you were."

"Do you know how many times someone has threatened to fire me?"

"Based on what I've seen so far, a lot."

"Some of my clients fire me ten or twenty times a day."

"Then I guess I've got a ways to go." Jude reached back and grabbed her hand, pulling her up beside him.

"Is the car still there?"

"Yeah."

"Let me see." She squeezed in closer, her hair brushing his chin as she jockeyed for a better position.

Jude pulled her up short, her wrist warm beneath his hand. For a moment he was back in the restaurant, Lacey's creamy skin peeking out from under her dark sweater, white scars criss-crossing the tender flesh. She'd shoved her sleeve down too quickly for him to get a good look, but the glimpse he'd gotten was enough. There was a lot more to Lacey then met the eye. A lot she hid behind a quick smile and a quicker wit. She'd been hurt before, and he wouldn't let it happen again. No way was he going to drag her into danger. Not now. Not tomorrow. Not ever. As soon as they got back to the house, he was going to do exactly what he'd threatened—fire her.

"It's not the car." She said it with such authority that Jude stepped from the shadows and took a closer look.

"Why do you say that?"

"The one back at the house had tinted glass. Really dark. This one, you can see in the back window. Looks like there is a couple sitting in the front seat. Unless you've got two people after you, I don't think that's the same car."

She was right.

Of course she was.

Jude could see inside the car, too, see the couple in the front seats. If he'd been thinking with his head instead of acting on the anger that had been simmering in his gut for months, he would have seen those things long before now. "You'd make a good detective, Lacey."

"You think so? Maybe I should make a career change. Give up home-care work for something more dangerous and exciting." She laughed as she pulled away from his hold and stepped out into the parking lot, but there was tension in her shoulders and in the air. As if she sensed the danger that had been stalking Jude, felt it as clearly as Jude did.

"I'm not sure being a detective is as dangerous or as exciting as people think. Most days it's a lot of running into brick walls.

Backing up, trying a new direction." He led Lacey across the parking lot, his body still humming with adrenaline.

"That sounds like life to me. Running into brick walls, backing up and trying new directions."

"True, but in my job the brick walls happen every other day. In life, they're usually not as frequent." He waited while she got into her car, then closed the door, glancing in the black sedan as he walked past. An elderly woman smiled and waved at him, and Jude waved back, still irritated with himself for the mistake he'd made.

Now that he was closer, it was obvious the two cars he'd seen weren't the same. The one at his place had been sleeker and a little more sporty. Which proved that when a person wanted to see something badly enough, he did.

"That wasn't much of a meal for you. Sorry to cut things short for a false alarm." He glanced at Lacey as he got in the Mustang and was surprised that her hand was shaking as she shoved the key in the ignition.

He put a hand on her forearm. "Are you okay?"

"Fine."

"For someone who is fine, your hands sure are shaking hard."

"How about we chalk it up to fatigue?"

"How about you admit you were scared?"

"Were? I still am." She started the car, and Jude let his hand fall away from her arm.

"You don't have to be. We're safe. For now."

"It's the 'for now' part that's got me worried. Who's trying to kill you, Jude? Why?"

"If I had the answers to those questions, we wouldn't be sitting here talking about it."

"You don't even have a suspect?"

"Lacey, I've got a dozen suspects. More. Every wife who's ever watched me cart her husband off to jail. Every son who's ever seen me put handcuffs on his dad. Every family member or friend who's sat through a murder trial and watched his or her loved one be convicted because of the evidence I put together."

"Have you made a list?

"I've made a hundred lists. None of them have done me any good. Until the person responsible comes calling again, I've got no evidence, no clues and no way to link anyone to the hit-and-run."

"Maybe he won't come calling again. Maybe the hit-and-run *was* an accident, and maybe the sedan we saw outside your house was just someone who got lost and ended up in the wrong place." She sounded like she really wanted to believe it.

He should let her, he thought. That was what he'd done with his family. Let them believe the hit-and-run was a fluke thing that had happened and was over. He'd done it to keep them safe. He'd do the opposite to keep Lacey from getting hurt.

"Have you ever walked outside at night?"

"Sure. Who hasn't?"

"Then you know how it feels to be at ease in the darkness. To feel like everything is just the way it should be."

"I guess. I've never really thought much about it."

"Imagine that you are outside, walking around, feeling like you have every other time. Next thing you know, your hair stands on end, your pulse starts racing and you realize you're being watched. You can't see the person, but you know he's there. And you know that as soon as you run, he's going to chase you down."

She stiffened, and Jude knew he had gotten through to her.

"That's what's going on with me, Lacey. That's how I know I'm in danger. I feel it."

"I can understand that." She sighed and brushed a strand of hair behind her ear.

"Then you'll also understand that as long as I'm in danger,

anyone who's near me is in danger, too. That's why you need to grab your suitcase and leave as soon as we get back to the house."

"I don't think so."

"What do you mean 'you don't think so'?"

"I mean, I've never left a job before my contract was up."

"There's a first time for everything."

"This won't be it."

"It will if you're carried out of here in a body bag."

"I don't think that is going to happen. The way I see it, God gave me this job for a reason. Until He tells me something different, I plan to keep it."

"God wouldn't want you to put yourself in danger to help me out."

"God expects us to do whatever job He gives us to the best of our abilities. That's what I plan to do."

"Sticking around is a bad idea."

"I don't think so."

"But you can't know."

"Sure I can. I feel it. The same way you feel danger breathing down your neck."

"Unfortunately for you, all the 'feeling' about it in the world isn't going to keep you working for me. I told you before that I was going to fire you. I wasn't kidding."

"Then I guess it's a good thing I'm working for your brother."

"You're working for Grayson for now. We'll see what tomorrow brings."

"Tomorrow is going to bring the sunrise. Just like it always does. As for anything else, I prefer to concentrate on today rather than worrying about what hasn't happened yet." She pulled out onto the road, her hands at precisely ten and two o'clock, her eyes trained on the road, tendrils of pale hair escaping her ponytail and sliding down her back. Delicate and pretty, Lacey wasn't the kind of woman Jude had ever paid much attention to. He preferred tall, athletic women. The kind who wouldn't hesitate to hike mountain trails or climb rock faces. The most strenuous thing he could imagine Lacey doing was sipping tea in a flower garden.

Despite that, or maybe because of it, he couldn't seem to pull his attention away from her.

That wasn't good.

Not when there were other, more important things he needed to focus on.

Like staying alive.

"There won't be a tomorrow if the guy who's after me decides two for one isn't a bad deal and takes you out at the same time."

"Why would he?"

"Murderers tend to get rid of witnesses. Unless you're in the market for dying in the next few days, you'd be much better off going back where you came from."

"Dying doesn't scare me. It's living that's hard." She stopped at a red light, tapping her fingers against the steering wheel.

"That's a morbid way of looking at things."

"Not when you've watched people suffer for weeks and months and even years. Most of my terminal clients fight and claw for more time, but eventually they accept that death isn't such a bad thing. It means freedom from pain, eternity with God. Once they embrace that, it doesn't scare them anymore."

"Maybe not, but that doesn't mean *you* shouldn't be scared. Dying of disease or age is one thing. Dying at the hands of another person is something else entirely."

"I didn't say I wasn't scared of being killed. I said I wasn't afraid of dying. One way or another, there's no way I'm going to walk away. I agreed to work for your brother. I signed a contract. More importantly, I believe this is where God wants me. Nothing is going to make me walk away from that."

She said it without heat, but Jude knew she meant it. In her eyes, a person did what she had to do. No matter how painful doing it might be.

"You're an interesting person, Lacey. Not easy to figure out."

"Why would anyone need to figure me out?" She pulled up in front of the house and shifted in her seat so she was facing him. The darkness hid her expression, painting shadows across her face and secrets in her eyes.

"Figuring someone out is part of getting to know them."

"Only if you're a bored homicide detective." She grinned, but there was no hiding her anxiety.

"Does it make you nervous that I want to find out more about you?"

"Why should it?"

"There you go again, avoiding my questions."

"I told you I didn't plan on answering them. The sun will be up in a few hours, so I guess it's time to stop playing twenty questions and get some sleep. I'll see you later." She was up the porch stairs and in her side of the duplex before Jude managed to get out of the car.

He grimaced, limping around the side of the car, his legs protesting every step. Light spilled onto the wide wheelchair ramp that Grayson had had built before Jude moved in. It was exactly the kind of thing Jude expected from his older brother, done out of love and concern, but serving only as a reminder of Jude's physical limitations.

He frowned, bypassing the ramp and using the stairs. It hurt, but not as much as rolling up the ramp in a wheelchair had. Yeah. He had a pride issue. He'd admit to it. But there were other reasons for using the stairs. He had to build his strength, regain his balance. Weakness made him vulnerable. There was no doubt the guy who was after him knew it.

He pushed open the front door and stepped into the duplex

his parents had insisted he use during his recovery. He'd have been just as happy to stay in New York. The chance of another attack occurring in the crowded city was a lot higher than the chance of it happening on the outskirts of Lynchburg, Virginia, and Jude had wanted it to happen, would have been happy to be a sitting duck in his studio apartment if it meant resolving the situation that much sooner.

If his mother hadn't threatened to stay with him there, he would have done just that. But there was no way he'd put her in danger. No way he wanted any of his family put in danger.

He lifted his laptop from the coffee table, booted it up and scanned the names he'd typed in earlier. Men and women. Young and old. He'd worked homicide long enough to know that no one could be ruled out. The list of possible suspects was long. Jude remembered many of the people listed on it. Loved ones who'd stood vigil during long trials. Some of them had been shocked, others sad. It was the ones who'd been angry and defiant who'd stuck in Jude's mind. Whether or not one of them was trying to kill him remained to be seen. It was possible the attempt on Jude's life had nothing to do with his job. In which case, investigating people connected to homicide cases might lead nowhere.

In the meantime, the clock was ticking and a killer was getting closer. Jude had tried to get his supervisor to step in and help with the investigation but had gotten a lukewarm response. Sure, Bill wanted to help, but he didn't want to expend time and money on something he deemed a wild goose chase.

So maybe it was time to head in a new direction.

Jude grabbed the phone, dialing quickly. It had been three weeks since he'd spoken to his ex-partner, Jackson Sharo. He should have returned some of his friend's phone calls before now, but hearing about Jack's work as a private investigator in New York only made Jude want what he couldn't have: his old life back.

The phone rang three times before Jackson answered. When he finally did, his voice was as raspy and old as a lifetime smoker's. "I thought about ignoring your call the way you've been ignoring mine, but then I wouldn't get the opportunity to tell what I think of you."

"Save it until after I apologize."

"You're calling me at four in the morning to apologize? Or are you planning to apologize for calling at four in the morning?"

"Both."

"Don't bother. We've known each other too long for either. So, what's up?"

"I need your help."

"Name it."

"I've got some legwork I need someone to do. Someone I trust."

"Go ahead."

"It's going to require some time, so you may want to hear me out before you agree. I know Laura's been on you to keep more reasonable hours."

"Laura and I split up three weeks ago."

Which Jude would have known if he'd bothered calling. The thought didn't make him feel any better about himself. He and Jackson had known each other for ten years. They'd both started in homicide the same year, had become partners six months later. Had gone camping and fishing in upstate New York every few months for as long as they'd known each other. They were as close as brothers. And a whole lot less judgmental of each other than blood brothers could be.

"I'm sorry, man. I thought you two were in it for the long haul."

"Yeah, well that was before we started planning the wedding and Laura realized that I didn't quite live up to her expectations."

"Like I said, I'm sorry."

"No, you're not. You never liked Laura."

"I liked her for about as long as it took me to get to know her."

"Me, too. Unfortunately, it took way too long for that to happen." Jackson laughed, but there was little humor in it. "You said you need some legwork. I've got the time. Tell me what you need me to do."

"I've got some people I want you to track down."

"People? How many are we talking about?"

"Twenty."

"You're kidding, right?"

"Would I be calling you at four in the morning to kid around?"

"The way you've been lately? No. So go ahead. Give me the list."

"You're not going to ask me why I need you to do this?"

"Man, I already know why. You're trying to find out who ran you down. You think maybe it wasn't an accident. You're convinced the accident had something to do with your job. Maybe a friend or relative of someone you put away."

"You've been talking to Bill."

"I have, but he didn't tell me anything I didn't already know. What you're thinking is exactly what I'd think if I were in your situation."

"I don't think anything, Jack. I know it. Someone is trying to kill me. I've noticed a black Honda following me around town. A few hours ago, it pulled into my driveway. Idled there until I tried to get a look at the driver. Then drove away."

"Did you get a license plate number?"

"No, but that doesn't mean the car wasn't there."

"Hey, no need to get defensive, man. I believe you. Give me the list. I'll see who's still in New York and who isn't."

"And you'll charge me your going rate."

"I'll charge you my family rate."

"You don't charge family."

"Exactly."

"Forget it, then. I'll hire someone else."

Jackson laughed again. This time, though, he sounded amused. "First of all, you wouldn't trust anyone else to do the job."

True, but Jude wasn't going to admit it.

"Second, I started my own list a few days after I spoke to Bill. So, whether you give me what you have or not, I'll still be pursuing the case. It'll just take me longer to figure things out. I don't know about you, but I've got a feeling your time is limited."

Jude had the same feeling, and wasting time arguing about whether or not Jackson was going to accept payment didn't make sense. "You win. I'll e-mail you the list and the information I've already gathered."

"I'll move on it today."

"Thanks, Jack." He saved the list of names as an attachment and sent it to his friend.

"You can thank me by watching your back. I'm not going to be happy if I have to search for another rock-climbing buddy."

"Looks like you're going to have to do that one way or another."

"You'll be back up those rock faces, Jude, if I have to drag your sorry behind the entire way." The line clicked, and Jude knew his friend was already working on the list he'd sent.

Maybe that would be enough, but Jude didn't think so. That same quiet voice that whispered of danger was telling him that Jackson's investigation might end up being too little too late, and that the death Jude had avoided for two months was biting at his heels, ready to take him down.

SIX

Lacey pulled her hair into a loose bun and eyed her reflection in the mirror. Nightmares had kept her awake half the night—or rather, half of what had been left of the night after they'd gotten home from the diner—and it showed. Dark circles. Pale lips. A frown line between her brows that hadn't been there yesterday.

Or had it?

She leaned closer, scowling at her reflection. She was too young to have lines and wrinkles and too old to be worried about them. Yet here she stood, staring at her reflection as if that could change anything.

She grabbed the keys from her dresser and hurried downstairs. She'd left all the lights on the previous night, and now went from room to room turning them off. Then checked the back door to make sure it was still locked, ran the vacuum she'd found in the coat closet, checked the thermostat, straightened a pillow that didn't need straightening.

And finally admitted the truth—she was avoiding doing what she knew she had to do. Her client was right next door and she was too chicken to walk the few feet that separated them, open his door and get to work.

Ten years of experience in her career, thirty-two clients attended to, and she was nervous.

Anxious.

Scared.

The feelings had churned in the pit of her stomach, filling her dreams and turning them into nightmares. Everything inside Lacey told her to pack her bag and run as fast and as far as she could. And not just because of Jude's belief that someone was trying to kill him. She'd faced danger before and wasn't about to let it force her to back down this time. But looking into Jude's eyes was like looking into a storm-filled sky. Beautiful and terrifying all at the same time.

If she were smart, she would run for cover.

She had always thought she was pretty smart.

So why wasn't she running?

She frowned and pulled open the front door. The rising sun bathed the front porch in watery light and tinged the lawn with gold. A few birds chirped happy greetings to one another and the cold air held the crisp, clean scent of winter. Lacey inhaled deeply, forcing herself to focus on the positive. A beautiful day. A job that paid well. A place to stay. Another day to enjoy it all. God had given her those things. If she really believed that, she also had to believe He'd brought her to Lynchburg for a purpose. If that was the case, she should stop worrying about Jude and his stormy gaze, stop worrying about the danger that seemed to hover just out of sight. Stop worrying and give it over to God, let Him be in control of it all.

If only that were as easy to do as it was to say.

She sighed, letting the cold morning seep into her bones. Not wanting to do what she knew she had to: turn around, knock on Jude's door and start her day. If he were any other client, it would be so easy. But he wasn't. He was Jude, and his deep-gray eyes seemed to look straight into her soul and see things Lacey would much rather keep hidden. Her past. All its darkness and fear.

Fingers of light painted the horizon golden pink, and Lacey

knew she couldn't put off the inevitable any longer. She took a deep breath, rapped her knuckles against the wood, waiting for a few heartbeats before she knocked again.

The door swung open and Jude glowered out at her, his dark hair damp, his eyes flashing with irritation. "It's seven in the morning."

"The perfect time to make a pot of coffee." She brushed by him, ignoring the heat that shot through her and the quick, wild thrum of her pulse as their arms touched.

"So make a pot over at your place. I'm busy."

"And bring it over here for you? It's much easier just to do it in your kitchen."

"You don't need to make me coffee. I can manage myself."

"Are you always this grumpy in the morning?" She walked into the kitchen, more aware than she wanted to be of Jude following along behind.

"Only when I've got an uninvited guest."

"Since I'm not a guest, we shouldn't have a problem." She plugged in his coffeemaker, and dumped the dregs from the pot. "Do you ever clean this thing out?"

"If I say no, will you go away?"

"No, but I'll clean it." She glanced at the pot—anything to avoid meeting his eyes. "I think I'll clean it anyway."

"You don't seem to get it, Lacey." He took the pot from her hand and set it on the counter, giving her no choice but to turn her attention from the job to the man. Big mistake.

He was even more handsome than she'd remembered, his eyes silver ice in a tan face.

"Get what?"

"I don't need you to clean out the coffeepot or make me coffee."

"Then I'll start on the dishes." She turned to the sink, but there was nothing in it. Apparently, he'd decided to clean since last night. "Or the laundry."

"You are *not* going to do my laundry."

"Why not?" She pushed open the laundry-room door, smiling at the pile of clothes thrown on the floor. Something to focus on. That was what she needed.

"Because I can manage myself."

"That's not what—"

"You were hired to do." He grabbed the back of her shirt as she stooped to scoop up the clothes. "Leave it, Lacey."

He sounded so serious, so determined, that Lacey straightened and turned to look in his eyes. Really look. Worry and anger made them stormy gray, but it was the pain in his gaze that caught and held Lacey's attention. It must have cost him a lot to walk down the stairs and open the door for her. She should have thought of that. Would have thought about it if Jude didn't throw her so off balance.

"How about we sit down and make a grocery list and go over your schedule. You've got physical therapy twice a week, right? And church. What other activities?" She sat at the table, hoping he would do the same.

She should have known he wouldn't. "No grocery list. No schedule. We're going next door, grabbing your suitcase and you're going to head out. That was the plan for the day. Remember?"

"That was *your* plan, Jude. I already told you I'm staying. I've been paid to do a job. I plan to do it." Since he wasn't sitting, she stood, grabbed the coffeepot and rinsed it.

"No job is worth your life."

"And yet you're a police detective who risks his life every day."

"That's different." He pulled coffee from a cupboard and handed it to Lacey. "You want some eggs?"

"Only if I make them."

"You think I can't cook?" He pulled eggs and milk from the fridge.

"I think you can probably do anything you set your mind to." She opened one cupboard after another until she found a bowl, her heart beating in a strange, hard rhythm that she couldn't ignore no matter how much she wanted to.

"If that's the case, then why are you sticking around?"

"Because it's obvious you don't want to do the things around this house that would make your life more comfortable."

"Like what?"

"The laundry, for one." She kicked at a spot of something on the floor. "The cleaning, for another."

"And you really think doing those things will make my life more comfortable?"

"Clean laundry, a clean house and hot coffee make life a *lot* more comfortable." Which was something Lacey had good reason to know and even more reason to appreciate. She started the coffee and cracked eggs in the bowl. "Scrambled?"

"Sure."

"And toast?"

"I'll do it." He put bread into the toaster and grabbed plates from the cupboard, moving in close as he worked, his arm pressing against Lacey's. She wanted to move away but didn't want to call attention to her discomfort. More than half of her clients had been men. There was no reason in the world why being so close to Jude should bother her.

"You seem tense." Jude pulled butter out of the refrigerator as he spoke, and if Lacey hadn't known better she would have thought he was just making an observation and expected no reply. She did know better. Jude was attuned to everything around him. Focused. Observant. Way too curious.

"Why would I be?"

"I don't know. I was hoping you'd fill me in."

"There's nothing to fill you in on."

When Jude didn't respond she turned to look at him, her heart skipping a beat as she met his eyes.

"I make you uncomfortable, Lacey. Why? You've been doing this kind of work for a decade. It seems to me you'd be over feeling uncomfortable around new clients."

He was so right it was scary, his words neatly expressing what she'd been thinking all morning. She didn't want to tell him that, though, and when his phone rang the sound offered her the perfect excuse to turn away from Jude's probing gaze.

She piled eggs onto both plates and set them down on the table. Then opened cupboards until she found coffee mugs. She knew she should go out in the living room and wait there until Jude finished his conversation. That would be the polite thing to do.

The right thing.

Of course, she didn't.

The eggs were perfectly cooked, the toast slathered with butter, the coffee hot. Why let good food go to waste?

She sat down, prayed and dug in, only half listening to Jude's conversation until he said a word that caught her full attention. *Murderer.* She inhaled sharply and choked on the bite of egg she'd just put in her mouth, coughing hard and grabbing her coffee. Nearly spilling it as Jude patted her back.

"Better watch it, Lacey. If you choke to death, my brother might think I had something to do with it."

"Not once the coroner found the egg lodged in my windpipe." She shifted beneath his hand, not comfortable with the warm weight of it on her back. Her job required a certain level of intimacy and often a measure of physical closeness, but as a rule Lacey was the one offering the pat on the back.

If Jude heard her comment, he ignored it, continuing his phone conversation as if she hadn't nearly choked on scrambled eggs. "Yeah. Murder one. According to the paper, his fiancée didn't believe it. She screamed curses at the jury after he was found guilty, but that doesn't mean she wants me dead. You said there's another possibility. Someone's wife?"

He paused, his hand dropping away from Lacey's back as he limped across the room and grabbed a bottle of Tylenol. He popped three tablets into his mouth, swallowed some water and then spoke into the phone again. "She didn't make any overt threats against me. Yeah. I know. It's as often the quiet, unassuming person who's a killer as it is the aggressive angry one." He glanced at Lacey and frowned.

"I hope you're not talking about me, because I'm not quiet and unassuming. I'm more the open-threat kind."

His lips quirked into a half smile, and he turned away, pacing to the back door and pushing it open. Cold air drifted into the kitchen as he disappeared outside; it swirled around Lacey's ankles and urged her to get up and follow him.

She didn't, of course. His conversation wasn't any of her business, and she had more important things to do. She took a final sip of coffee, searched Jude's cupboards for plastic wrap and covered his food. She'd heat it up in the microwave when he returned.

Until then, she'd take a peek in his fridge and cupboards to make a list of what he had and what it looked like he needed, and then start his laundry. He may have said he didn't need her help, but the pile she'd seen on the floor said otherwise. Besides, keeping busy was the best way to keep her mind off the things that had kept her tossing and turning when she'd tried to sleep. Murder. Mystery. Men. Jude, to be exact.

And her past.

Which was something she didn't like to spend any time at all thinking about.

"So why are you? It's not like there aren't plenty of other things to set your mind to." She pulled open the refrigerator door and frowned at the contents. A half gallon of milk, a stick of butter and a few covered Tupperware containers. "This isn't much of a choice for a man who is trying to regain his health."

"Do you make a habit of talking to yourself?" Jude stepped back into the house and closed the door, the quiet click of it reminding Lacey that she was alone with a man who seemed to see much more than any other ever had.

"Only when there's no one else to talk to."

"And do you also make a habit of looking through other people's refrigerators?"

"Only when they're not around to stop me." She grinned, enjoying the lighthearted banter more than she wanted to admit. "By the way, you don't have enough food in there to feed a mouse."

"I suppose you want me to do something about that." He grabbed his coffee cup and topped it off, then took the plate of food Lacey was lifting from the table, putting it in the microwave before she could.

"It would make sense. I mean, you can't rebuild your strength with eggs, coffee and toast."

"Trust me. I've been eating more than that. The ladies at my mother's church have been generous." He sent a wry smile in her direction and shoved the covered plate into the microwave. "So, listen, I've got a job for you."

"Sorry, but I've already been hired by someone else."

"We've already established that I don't need you hanging around the house getting in the way."

"I do *not* get in the way."

"Okay. You don't get in the way, but I don't need you here, either."

"So where *do* you need me?"

"Running some errands."

That sounded simple enough, but Lacey was pretty certain it wasn't. "What kind of errands?"

"No need to sound so suspicious. All I need you to do is run into town and get me a few things."

"What things?"

"There you go, sounding suspicious again." He grinned, but Lacey didn't miss the calculation in his eyes. He was sizing her up, checking to see if she'd buy what he was trying to sell.

"And there you go again not telling me what kind of errands you're sending me on."

He chuckled and limped into the living room, ignoring the beep of the microwave and the food that was waiting for him. "It's nothing dangerous or illegal, Lacey. I just need a couple of three-ring binders, some notebook paper and a three-hole punch. And a six-pack of root beer."

It seemed like an odd list, but Lacey nodded, grabbing a piece of paper from Jude's printer and a pen from the coffee table. "Okay, some three-ring binders, notebook paper, three-hole punch, root beer."

"You can throw in a box of Twinkies while you're at it. Some razors. Any brand. Maybe price some big-screen television sets. The one here is too small."

She glanced up from the paper, met his silvery eyes. "You don't look like someone who spends a lot of time watching television."

"I wasn't before. I am now."

She frowned, searching his face for a clue as to what was going on. There was no way Jude had suddenly changed his mind about needing her help, and there was no way a man like him really wanted a big-screen TV. Mountain climbing, hiking, camping. Those were the things she could picture him doing. She couldn't picture him camped out in front of a television set watching hours of sitcoms and dramas. "What's going on, Jude? And don't feed me another line about wanting me to run errands."

"You've got me all wrong, Lacey. If I were going to feed you a line, I'd say something like this." He moved close, touching her cheek with fingers that were rough and calloused, holding her in place with the sheer force of his gaze. "When I saw you for the first time, I thought you were a fairy-tale princess come to life. Then I looked in your eyes and saw the determination and strength in them, and knew you were something even better. A flesh-and-blood woman. Someone with passion and integrity. Someone I wanted to get to know."

Okay.

He was right.

That was a line. And a good one, because it was exactly the kind of thing Lacey would have wanted a man to say to her if she'd been interested in dating. Thank goodness she wasn't. "Look, Jude, whatever you're planning, you're not going to hide it from me by offering distractions."

"I'm planning to eat breakfast."

And something else.

Something that he had no intention of telling Lacey about.

Lacey was sure of that; she just wasn't sure she should do anything about it. Grayson had hired her to help around Jude's house, run errands for him, make sure he got to appointments and to church if his legs were too weak or painful for him to be able to drive himself.

Keeping Jude from doing something foolish wasn't written into the terms of the contract. Whatever he wanted to do, it wasn't her place to stop him.

"All right. I'll get my purse and be on my way."

She walked out of the kitchen and opened the door, ready to put some distance between herself and Jude. A little fresh air. A little time. She'd put the job back into perspective.

"Hold on a minute, Lacey." Jude wrapped a hand around her bicep, pulling her to a stop. "I'm going to do some gardening soon. There's a great nursery about twenty minutes from here. Maybe you can pick up some plants."

"You're going to garden?" She gritted her teeth to keep from telling Jude what she thought of his endless list of errands.

"Isn't that what all invalids do? Putter around in their gardens and make things grow?" He flashed his teeth in a feral smile that didn't make Lacey feel any better about the errands she was about to run.

"Apparently it's what *you're* going to do. I'll see you in a couple of hours." She took her time going into her house and grabbing her purse. There was no real hurry. There was nothing on Jude's list that he really needed and no reason for Lacey to rush. Besides, she was curious, and more than a little concerned. No matter how many times she told herself it was none of her business, she wanted to know why Jude was trying to get her away from his house.

Did he have an assignation with the murderer?

Had he somehow found out who the person was?

Or was he planning to go off on his own, hunting for a killer who was probably much better prepared to fight than Jude?

The thought didn't sit well with her, and Lacey frowned as she stepped back outside.

Was Jude going after the killer?

The question lingered in the air, following Lacey into her car and down the driveway. The answer was obvious—of course he was. Why else would he be so determined to get her out of the house and away from him? An image of Jude lying bleeding and still filled Lacey's mind, and she blanched. No way could she let him go after a killer alone. She opened Bess's glove compartment and pulled out a chocolate bar. Nothing like a little sugar to get the mind working properly. Too bad it couldn't also give her superhuman strength and the ability to stop bullets. Lacey sighed and shook her head. The way she saw it, she had two choices. Go or stay. Which was really no choice at all.

She pulled onto the main road, found a place to park the car and finished off her candy bar. She wasn't sure what kind of vehicle Jude drove, but since his was the only house at the end of the driveway, she'd just wait until she saw him pull onto the road and follow.

Of course, if the murderer parked somewhere else and walked to the duplex, Lacey would be sitting in Bess nibbling chocolate while Jude fought for his life.

Not a good plan.

It would be better to get out of the car and walk back to the house. Keep an eye on things from the woods that surrounded the property. If Jude got in his car and tried to leave, Lacey would throw herself in front of his car and pray he didn't run her over.

It was a much more dramatic plan than sitting in the car and waiting, but Lacey decided to go with it. Anything was better than sitting in the car wondering what was going on back at Jude's place.

She grabbed another chocolate bar from the glove compartment, zipped her coat and slipped into the woods, praying she wasn't walking into the biggest mistake of her life.

SEVEN

Jude waited until Lacey drove out of sight before stepping back into the house. She'd known he didn't need any of the things he'd asked her to get and hadn't been happy about the errands, but Jude didn't care. Jackson had called an hour ago. Morgan Bradshaw, the wife of a man Jude had put in jail for second-degree murder, was living twenty-five miles away in the small town of Lakeview. She'd moved there a week after Jude's accident.

A coincidence?

Jude didn't think so.

He walked to the computer and turned it on, smiling when he saw the address Jackson had e-mailed him. There was no need to map it; he knew the street. Had spent a good amount of time in Lakeview when he was a kid. Riding bikes. Swimming in the lake. Hanging out with friends.

In a half hour he might be standing face-to-face with the person who'd nearly killed him. There was no way he was going to have Lacey with him when that happened. Anyone crazy enough to mow down another human being wouldn't hesitate to take out an innocent bystander.

He grabbed his coat and wallet, strapped on his holster and headed out back. A large garage stood outside the fenced-in yard. Jude opened the back gate, entered the garage and unlocked his Mustang convertible. Not the best ride for someone with injuries like his, but Jude hadn't been willing to give it up.

Apparently Lacey liked her Mustang just as much. Her car needed a major overhaul, but she defended it like it was her baby.

Funny that they both had Mustangs.

Not so funny that he was thinking about Lacey and her car when he had a murderer to find.

He frowned, pulling a lawn mower out of the garage and to the side of the building. The cold winter air held a hint of moisture and the latent promise of spring. It wouldn't be long before the trees blossomed and flowers bloomed, before birds greeted each day and crickets bid it good-night. Jude planned to be around when that happened. He couldn't allow himself to be distracted. Not by anyone.

Something rustled in the trees near the edge of the property, and he dove for cover, hitting the ground with a thud that knocked the breath from his lungs and sent pain shooting through his legs. Stars danced in front of his eyes, and only sheer force of will kept him conscious.

He pulled his gun, aiming in the direction of the sound. Waiting. Listening. Someone was there, just out of sight behind the heavy foliage. He was sure of it.

"I know you're there. Come out before I decide to shoot first and ask questions later."

A moment passed before the leaves rustled again. A figure stepped out into the sunlight. Golden hair twisted into a loose bun, tendrils of it escaping and hanging in long strands against her neck. Green eyes that glowed in the sunlight. Dark turtle-neck and faded jeans.

Lacey.

Of course.

Anger brought Jude to his feet too quickly, and he nearly

toppled over again. But there was no way would he let himself go down. Not before he told Lacey just how foolish she'd been. He could have shot her! She could be lying bleeding, dying in the woods.

He strode across the yard, anger masking his pain and making movement easier. "What do you think you're doing?"

He nearly shouted the question, and Lacey paled, taking a quick step back. "Checking to make sure you were okay."

"By hiding in the bushes and spying on me?" He grabbed her hand before she could back up again, pulling her so close he could see the flecks of brown and blue in her eyes and the gold that tinged the ends of her thick eyelashes.

"I wasn't hiding or spying." She scowled, but her voice shook, and Jude knew she was as scared as he'd been when he'd seen her walk out of the woods.

Good.

That was what he wanted.

It was the only way to keep her safe.

"Then what *were* you doing? Because from where I was standing, hiding and spying is what it looked like."

"I was just…" Her voice trailed off and she shrugged. "Okay, so maybe I *was* hiding. I was walking down the driveway and heard you go out your back door. I wanted to see what you were doing. Which, I guess if you want to look at it that way, was spying." She tugged to free her hand, but Jude held tight, anger still raging through him.

She could have died.

He could have been her killer.

"Do you realize how stupid that was? I could have shot you!"

"There's no need to shout, Jude. I'm a half inch from your face." She pulled against his hold again and a vivid picture flashed through Jude's mind. Pale skin crisscrossed with old scars. Thin, ropey evidence of something that had happened years ago.

He loosened his grip, smoothed his hand over the tender flesh. "Okay. I'm not shouting. I'm asking. What were you thinking?"

"I was thinking you might need my help. I was thinking I should make sure you were okay." Her voice broke, and Jude stilled, his chest tight with fear and anger and something else. Something that made him want to pull Lacey into his arms, tell her everything was going to be okay.

"I'm a thirty-four-year-old man. I don't need checking up on, Lacey." He did what he needed to, pulling her into his arms, letting his hands rest on the slender curve of her waist.

She tensed, but didn't pull away.

"You could have died. You know that, right?"

She shook her head, easing away, putting distance between them that Jude didn't want. "You wouldn't have fired a shot into the bushes without seeing who was there. We both know that."

"You're right. But someone else—"

"There was no one else here. Just us. Look." She paused, running a hand through her hair and staring into the woods. "I'm sorry if I scared you. I was just trying to do my job."

"Your job is to run those errands for me."

"Why? So you could go off and find a killer by yourself?"

"If that's what I've got planned, it's my business. Not yours."

"You're wrong. As long as your brother is employing me, everything you do is my business."

"Maybe that's the way it worked with your other clients, but it's not the way it works with me. I've got somewhere to go. You can't come. Period."

"You know I'm going to follow you, right? So you may as well just give in and let me come along."

"By the time you get back to your car, I'll be long gone."

She frowned. "Not if I run."

"Even if you run." He got in the car, started the engine. "Back up, Lacey. I don't want to run over your feet."

She took a step back, frowning, her eyes flashing with green fire. "I guess I'm not as brave as I thought."

"What do you mean by that?" He paused with his hand on the door, curious and knowing he shouldn't be. What he *should* have been was halfway down the driveway already.

"I had this scene all planned out in my mind. You'd be driving away, and I'd throw myself in front of your car to stop you. Now that I'm here and it's happening, I'm not sure that's the best idea I've ever had."

"Sorry to hear it."

"I guess I'll have to come up with a plan B."

"Good luck with that." Amused, Jude closed the door, rolling down the window when Lacey knocked on the glass. "What?"

"I've got my plan B worked out."

"You're fast on your feet."

"You want to hear it?"

"I already know it. You're going to call Grayson. Go ahead. By the time he figures out where I've gone, I'll already be done with what needs doing. See you later." He took his foot off the brake, let the car roll forward.

Lacey jumped back, a frown pulling at her soft lips. She looked unhappy but undefeated. Jude had the sudden image of her bursting through a window at Morgan Bradshaw's house and throwing herself in front of a bullet meant for him. Another one followed on its heels—Grayson breaking down the door and walking into a death trap. If Lacey called Jude's brother, if Morgan were a murderer, if the timing worked out just right.

Too many ifs and no guarantees.

Except for one. If Jude left Lacey, she'd call Grayson and then she'd try to follow. If things worked out the wrong way, someone could die.

He stepped on the brake, scowled at Lacey. "You want to

come, come, but we're playing by my rules, not yours. What I say goes. You understand?"

"Sure."

"I mean it, Lacey. More than likely, what I'm doing won't be dangerous, but if it is, I don't want you getting in the way."

"I won't. I promise."

She sounded like a grade-school kid, all earnest enthusiasm, and Jude's stomach twisted. "Maybe this isn't such a good idea."

"It's a great idea. I'll drive and you can navigate."

"*I'm* driving. You sit and be quiet."

She was in the car before he could finish the sentence, buckling her seat belt like the good citizen she was. "You don't have your seat belt on."

"And?"

"Surely you know how important that can be if you're in an accident." She reached over, her hand brushing against his chest and shoulder as she reached for his seat belt, her hair sliding against his cheek.

"I'll get it." He gave her a gentle nudge back toward her seat and clicked his seat belt into place, his pulse pounding hot and quick as the scent of rain and flowers enveloped him.

"I've been thinking that after we run this errand, we can go to the Booker T. Washington National Monument. According to your case file, your physical therapist wants you to take a walk every day. The trails at the park are supposed to be easy walking and a lot more fun than taking a few laps around your house."

"What else does the case file say about me?"

"Nothing you wouldn't be willing to tell me yourself."

"Why do I not believe that?"

"Because you've got a suspicious nature. So, how about that walk?"

"Do you realize the kind of trouble we could be heading into?"

"I'm doing my best not to think about it."

"If you're scared, I can let you out at your car."

"The worst thing a person can do is let fear get the better of her. So I think I'll stay right where I am."

"And plan walks instead of thinking about danger?"

"It works for me."

"It won't if we get where we're going and you decide you need to throw yourself in front of a bullet for me."

"Why would I do something like that?"

"Because you think it's in your job description?" He glanced her way, but she was staring out the window, the curve of her jaw and the delicate line of her neck making Jude want to turn the car around and forget about going to see Morgan Bradshaw until he had Lacey locked up somewhere safe.

"Look, if bullets fly, I'll cower behind something and call for help."

"There won't be any need for cowering because you'll be waiting in the car."

"But—"

"It's that, or I can't bring you. If something happened to you, I'd never forgive myself."

"I'm touched that you're so concerned."

Surprised, he glanced her way again, sure he'd see mockery in her face.

Instead, he looked into eyes filled with sincerity.

And he wanted to keep looking, wanted to see more, figure out what secrets hid in the depths of her gaze.

He jerked his attention back to the road, refusing to acknowledge what he'd been looking for. What he'd almost thought he'd seen. The same thing he'd looked for in the eyes of every woman he'd ever dated. Looked for, but never found.

Forever.

I knew your mother was the woman for me when I looked into her eyes and saw forever.

The words still echoed through Jude's mind twenty-three years after his father had said them. At nearly thirty-four, Jude was pretty sure he should have forgotten them by now. For some reason, though, they'd stuck.

"You're smiling." Lacey pulled him from his thoughts and Jude shrugged.

"Just thinking about something my father told me a long time ago."

"What?"

"That I'd know a woman was the right one when I looked into her eyes and saw forever."

"Your father is a romantic."

"Not even close. Maybe that's why his words have stuck with me for so long."

"So? Have you ever seen forever in a woman's eyes?"

He'd seen something shimmering in the depth of Lacey's eyes. The hint of a promise he hadn't ever believed in.

"Not yet, and I'm not holding out hope that I will. How about you?"

"Seen forever in a man's eyes? I haven't even seen two minutes." She laughed.

"I guess you just haven't met the right man."

"There is no right one, Jude. At least, not for me. I learned a long time ago that my life was a whole lot easier when I didn't have a man in it."

"Someone hurt you."

"There isn't a person alive who hasn't been hurt."

"Who was it?" He pictured her scarred wrists, imagining all the ways she could have been injured and wanted to get his hands on the person who'd done it.

"Not anyone who matters anymore. The way I see things,

it isn't what happens to someone that matters. It's how it changes her. What happened to me made me stronger. That's what's important."

"You didn't answer my question."

"Sure I did. It just wasn't the answer you wanted." Her tone was light, her fingers tapping softly against her thigh.

She wanted the conversation to end, and Jude knew it wasn't his right to keep it going. Lacey was his brother's employee. She was a woman who would be out of his life in less than a month. She was trouble.

What she was *not* was forever.

He needed to keep that in mind. If he didn't, his life might get a whole lot more complicated than it already was.

And that, he knew, could be dangerous for them both.

EIGHT

Forever in a man's eyes?

Lacey nearly snorted as the words danced through her mind again. As if that were a possibility. As if she would even want to look. Forever wasn't for her. Family. Connections. Home. She'd given up on those things when she was seventeen, and she'd never looked back.

Wouldn't look back.

She had friends. She had faith. She didn't need or want more than that.

Liar.

You want more. You just know you won't get it.

Okay, so maybe that was true.

A small part of her did want something more than what she had. After ten years of moving from assignment to assignment, Lacey longed for a place to call home. And sometimes, if she let herself, she longed for someone to come home to. A gentle embrace. Someone who cared.

"Are you okay?" Jude's hand rested on hers, the warmth of it seeping deep into her bones and chasing away the chill Lacey hadn't realized she was feeling.

"Of course. Why do you ask?"

"Because you're quiet. And in the few hours I've known you,

you have yet to be quiet for more than a few seconds." There was laughter in his words, and Lacey smiled, deciding to enjoy the moment.

"I'm not sure, but I think you just insulted me."

"I never said that talking was a bad thing. I was just commenting on the fact that you do it a lot."

"And you don't do it enough. You still haven't told me where we're going." She moved the conversation onto less personal ground.

"A little town called Lakeview. It's right on Smith Mountain Lake. Ever heard of it?"

"Only when I was researching things to do in the area. I saw pictures. It looked beautiful."

"It is. When I was a kid, we boated and water-skied there all the time."

"And now we're going to try to find a criminal there."

"I'm going to question a woman whose husband I put in jail. That doesn't mean she's a criminal. It just means I want to know why she's in Lakeview."

"Don't worry, Jude. I know enough not to rush in and accuse the woman of attempted murder."

"I'm sure you do, but it's a moot point. You're not rushing in anywhere. You're sitting in the car while I ask the questions."

"Really? I must have missed the memo."

"No memo was necessary. I agreed to bring you with me if you played by my rules. This is my rule—you stay in the car."

"Unless you need my help."

"I won't."

"You might."

Jude sighed. "You know what? You remind me of my sister."

"Your sister?" She should have been glad he was thinking of her in a fraternal way. So why wasn't she? Lacey wasn't sure she was willing to admit the answer to that question.

"Yeah. She's the baby in the family. Used to getting her way."

"Then we're nothing alike."

"No?"

"I wasn't the baby of the family. And I never got my way." Her life had been work and more work, but nothing she'd done had ever been enough. Not for her mother. Certainly not for her stepfather.

"Interesting."

"What?"

"I think that's the first piece of information I've gotten about your life that I haven't had to pull out of you."

"I don't think that makes it interesting."

"Sure it does. It brings me a little closer to figuring out who you are."

"You already know who I am, and we decided there was no need to figure me out."

"You decided that. I'm still curious."

He cast a long look in her direction, and Lacey braced herself for more questions about her past. Instead, Jude turned onto a narrow, tree-lined street and pointed to a bungalow-style house with a sign in front of it. "That's where we're heading."

"It's a pottery studio."

"It's also where Morgan Bradshaw lives. I helped get her husband convicted of second-degree murder three months ago."

"Who did he kill?"

"A business partner who apparently had designs on Morgan. Or so his story went."

"You didn't believe him?"

"I don't believe anyone, Lacey. Not until I have facts to substantiate what they're saying." He pulled up in front of the old house and idled at the curb, maybe reading the sign.

To the left, a parking lot had been created out of what had probably once been an empty lot.

Jude pulled into it, stopping beside an orange Jeep.

"Are you sure she lives here?" Lacey craned her neck to see past Jude.

"My friend Jackson says she does. I've known him to be wrong about something like this."

"How long have you known him?"

"Ten years."

Too bad. Lacey had hoped there was some room for error. She scanned the yard, not knowing what she was looking for. The place looked well tended, but the yard was as impersonal as the white sign with its plain blue letters.

Clay Treasures.

A generic name for a place that was neither flowery nor pretty. No curtains in the windows, not on the lower level, anyway. Upstairs, in what would have been the attic, a window was framed by white eyelet curtains. "Maybe she lives upstairs."

"She might. Or maybe we've got the wrong place. I'm going to find out." Jude got out of the car, and Lacey did the same, falling into step beside him.

He looked into her eyes, a puzzled frown carving lines beside his mouth. "I thought we agreed you were staying in the car."

"That was before we knew we were going to a very public place. I love pottery."

"And when did you discover this?"

"About three seconds after we pulled into the parking lot."

His laughter made Lacey smile. How Jude had managed to chase four previous home-care aides away, she didn't know. He was funny and smart and not nearly as demanding as some of the other clients Lacey had worked with.

"So you're going to look at pottery while I question Mrs. Bradshaw?"

"Among other things."

"What other things?"

"Maybe I'll talk to some of the people that shop there. See if they've been in before. If they have, they might be able to tell me a little about your suspect."

"Hold on a minute, Nancy Drew." He stopped and turned to face her. "I don't want you asking anybody any questions. This is a small town and people talk. If Morgan is a murderess, that's fine. If she's just someone trying to start a new life for herself, it isn't. If people around town start wondering about her past or why she's here, who knows what kind of stories they'll spread."

"All right. So I'll just look at pottery." And listen in on Jude's conversation with Morgan Bradshaw. She wasn't Nancy Drew, but Lacey was a good judge of character. She'd had to be. There'd been too many people in her life who had pretended to be one thing when they were really something else.

"Just look at pottery, huh?"

"Sure."

"Fine. You can come with me as long as you keep quiet. Deal?"

"Deal."

"That was almost too easy." He smiled and took her hand, his grip firm and strong as he led her to the shop. It wasn't the first time she'd held hands with a client, but for some reason, holding hands with Jude felt different. *She* felt different. Her heart beat just a little too fast, her hand tingled where it touched Jude's. If she didn't know better, she'd think she was attracted to the man. She did know better. To prove it, she pulled her hand from his and hurried up the steps. The gallery door was double-wide and stained deep mahogany. Lacey pushed it open and stepped into a brightly lit room.

The outside of Clay Treasures might have been plain, but the inside was beautiful. Pedestals and shelves housed dozens of pottery designs. Teapots and vases, bowls and cups and some abstract forms that swooped and swirled and wrapped around themselves. The figures were strange and intriguing, something that Lacey imagined she might put on a table in the foyer of a house. If she ever owned a house that had a big enough foyer for a table.

"Can I help you?" A young woman walked toward Lacey, a smile easing the sharp angles of her too-thin face. Almond-shaped eyes tilted up at the corners, their cornflower-blue contrasting sharply with the woman's tan skin.

"We're looking for Morgan Bradshaw." Jude walked into the shop and joined Lacey, his hand resting on her shoulder as he glanced around the room.

"I'm Morgan. What can I do for you?"

"*You're* Morgan?" Jude sounded as surprised as Lacey felt. Though why she was surprised, Lacey didn't know. She really hadn't thought about what the woman would look like. Nor had she bothered to envision the face of a killer. Somehow, though, Morgan's delicate elfin features and tip-tilted eyes made her seem much too delicate to be a criminal.

"Yes. And you're Detective Sinclair. I remember you from my husband's trial." She didn't ask why he was there, and Lacey wondered if she already knew.

"Funny, but I don't remember seeing you there. The Mrs. Bradshaw I remember was about two hundred pounds heavier than you, with red hair and brown eyes."

"That was Toby's sister, Anna. She came in for the trial."

"She spent most of the time crying into a tissue."

"She was sure he was innocent."

"Were you?"

She shrugged, turning away from Jude and not answering his question as she straightened a few vases that sat on a table.

"Is this your place?"

At Jude's next question, she turned back to face him, and

Lacey could see the unease in her eyes. She didn't look guilty of anything, but she did look scared. "Yes. I've always wanted my own place. This seemed like the perfect time to give it a shot."

"Is it a perfect time because your husband is in jail?"

"He's my ex-husband, Detective. The divorce was finalized two months ago."

"Around the same time you moved here."

"I'm sure you didn't come here to exchange idle chitchat, so why *are* you here?" She sidestepped the issue.

"I'm just wondering why a woman from New York City came all the way to Lakeview, Virginia, to open a shop."

"Cheap rent." She smiled and waved as an older woman walked into the shop. "I've got those bowls all set for you, Mrs. Smithfield. I'll wrap them up in just a moment."

"No hurry, my dear. I want to take a look around. My daughter's birthday is next week. I may pick something out for her." The elderly woman wandered farther into the shop, and Morgan turned her attention back to Jude.

"Look, I don't want to be rude, but I've got a business to run. Unless you've got something specific you're here for, I really don't have time for chitchat."

"Like I said, I was curious."

"You know what they say about curiosity, Detective."

"Is that a threat?"

"Why would I threaten you?" She looked surprised, her dark brows pulling together, and Lacey felt sorry for her. Jude had an agenda. The poor woman just hadn't realized it yet.

"Because I put your husband in jail."

"Ex-husband. And he put himself in jail."

"I couldn't agree more, but I still think it odd that you're here in the town I spent a lot of my childhood in. A town where some of my family lives." Jude smiled, but it looked more feral than friendly.

Morgan must have noticed, because she stiffened, her face going pale. "I don't know what your game is, Detective—"

"No game. I just want to know how you ended up so close to my family."

"You want the truth?"

"It would be a pleasant change."

"Jude—" Lacey tried to intervene, but neither Jude nor Morgan paid her any attention.

"I heard you talking before court started one day. You mentioned Smith Mountain Lake and said you were heading down here for some fishing as soon the trial was over."

"So you decided to move here?"

"The name stuck in my head." She shrugged, moved to the checkout counter at the back of the shop and started wrapping a cobalt-blue bowl. "After Toby went to jail, I needed to find a place where I could put the past behind me. I did some Internet searches, looking for a small town to settle in, but I couldn't find what I was looking for. One day, I just typed in Smith Mountain Lake. I fell in love with the pictures and came for a visit the next day."

"And the rest is history?"

"Something like that." She wrapped another bowl.

"I see."

"I don't think you do, Detective. I came here to escape my past. If I'd had any idea that I might run into you, I would have stayed far away. I knew you fished at the lake, but that's far enough from my shop that I didn't have any worries we'd see each other. Now that we have, I can't say it's changed anything. I like it here. I plan to stay."

"I'm not asking you to leave, Mrs. Bra—"

"Actually, it's Morgan Alexandria now."

"Ms. Alexandria, then. I'm not here to cause trouble. I just wanted the truth about why you were here."

"Now you have it. Feel free to leave."

"And miss taking a look at what your shop has to offer? My mother's birthday is coming up. Maybe I'll buy her a vase or a teapot." He smiled the same quick curve of the lips that always seemed to steal Lacey's breath.

Did he practice it in front of the mirror?

She wanted to believe Jude was vain and manipulative enough to do just that, but she knew the truth. Jude's rugged good looks weren't something he worked on. Too bad. If they had been, he would have been a lot less likeable.

"You're welcome to look around, Detective. But I'm not answering any more questions." Morgan turned away, apparently not nearly as affected by Jude's smile as Lacey was.

"I guess that's that." Lacey took a step toward the door, but Jude didn't follow. She turned, frowning and gesturing toward the door, hoping he'd get the hint.

If he did, he ignored it.

Instead of walking outside, he moved into the middle of the room, his gaze searching the pottery display as if he could find more answers hidden amidst the art pieces. At the back of the gallery, Morgan wrapped two more blue bowls and shot an angry look in Jude's direction.

Obviously, she wanted Jude to leave as much as Lacey did.

"You know she's not going to tell you any more, right?" Lacey whispered the question, and Jude nodded.

"I think I'll just take a look around. And my mother's birthday really is coming up." He walked to the counter where Morgan worked, smiling warmly at the elderly woman who held a narrow yellow vase. "That's a beautiful vase, ma'am."

"Isn't it? And those bowls!" She sighed deeply. "Aren't they beautiful? I'm just tickled pink that Morgan was able to make them for me. She had a set of pale-green bowls, but I truly needed to have blue bowls to go with the blue walls in my dining room. I'm one of Morgan's troublesome customers. Aren't I, dear?"

"Not at all, Mrs. Smithfield. I was happy to make a new set of bowls for you."

"You're too kind, but we both know the truth. That's the second set of blue bowls Morgan has created for me. The first set wasn't as true of a blue. It had just a touch of green in it, and I just couldn't have that, not when everything in my dining room is blue."

"Of course you couldn't, ma'am." Jude sounded amused, but Lacey was sure he was filing away every bit of the conversation. Later he'd take it out and go over it, try to figure out if he'd missed something important.

Lacey, on the other hand, was trying to think of a graceful way to get him moving. The sooner they left Morgan's shop, the happier she'd be. She and Jude might not be in any danger, but Lacey was afraid the detective and the shop owner might not stay civil for much longer.

"Jude, did you want to take a look at those teapots for your mom?"

"Sure."

"Oh, the teakettles. They are lovely, aren't they? I'm particularly fond of the red-and-orange one with the rooster head on the handle." Mrs. Smithfield nearly gushed with enthusiasm, and Lacey smiled.

"It's interesting." But not something Lacey would ever buy.

"Truly. Unfortunately, it isn't one of Morgan's, and I'm only buying her work."

"There's no reason why you can't buy the rooster pot. I know Paige would be happy to hear that you've purchased it," Morgan cut in, her gaze still on Jude. If looks could kill, Lacey was sure he'd be dead by now.

"No. I just couldn't. However, perhaps this young man and

his wife would like to buy it. You're newlyweds, right? All new-lyweds need something frivolous and fun. Like that teapot."

Newlyweds?

Lacey and Jude?

She would have laughed at the idea if she hadn't been so busy turning three shades of red. "We're not—"

"We're picking out something for my mother's birthday." Jude stepped in, smoothly turning the conversation in a new direction.

"She's a lucky woman, then, to have a son that is willing to shop in a boutique for her birthday gift rather than in a super-market. My own sons are content to buy me toasters and oven mitts every year. Not that I'm not grateful, but this…" She waved her hand toward the gallery. "If they shopped here, I'd be thrilled."

"Here you go, Mrs. Smithfield. You're all wrapped up and ready to go." Morgan nudged a large, double-handled paper bag toward the older woman.

"Thank you, dear." She lifted it, frowning a little as she took a step away. "I think I must have bought too many pieces. This is much heavier than I expected."

"Why don't I take it for you?" Jude lifted the bag from her hands, and Lacey wondered if he was doing it because he wanted to get information out of the woman, or because he was a gentleman. She had a feeling it was a little of both.

"Oh, I couldn't ask you to do that—"

"You're not asking. I'm volunteering. It'll only take a few minutes of my time."

"Well, if you're sure…"

"I'm sure. You're parked in the parking lot?"

"Yes. The Crown Victoria. Goodbye, Morgan. I'll see you in a week or so."

"See you then." Morgan smiled at the older woman. "Good-bye, Detective."

"I'm not leaving yet. I still have to pick a gift for my mother. Do you mind waiting here and taking a look around for me, Lacey?"

She did, but she couldn't say it. Not in front of Morgan or Mrs. Smithfield. "Not at all."

"Thanks." He moved toward the exit with only a slight limp, his voice a quiet rumble as he opened the door for the older woman and ushered her outside.

Which left Lacey alone with Morgan.

Obviously, Jude had a reason for leaving her there. Too bad she didn't know what it was.

She took a deep breath and did the only thing she could— asked to see a blue-and-gray teapot that was sitting on a shelf behind Morgan.

Lord willing, Jude would be back long before Lacey had to admit that she knew nothing about pottery and nearly nothing about shopping for gifts for someone's mother.

NINE

Jude knew walking Mrs. Smithfield to her car would take longer than a few minutes. He'd known plenty of women like her when he'd lived in Lynchburg, and not one of them passed up a chance at a long conversation. Mrs. Smithfield was the kind of woman who was both sweet-natured and strongly opinionated. Older, set in her ways, but with a soft spot for the underdogs in life. And Morgan did seem to be that.

Which, Jude had to admit, was a disappointment.

He'd been picturing the large red-haired woman he'd seen at Toby Bradshaw's trial and had almost convinced himself she was the murderer. When he'd seen Morgan, he'd been surprised. It was a feeling he didn't like.

What he liked even less was the instinct telling him that Morgan had nothing to do with the hit-and-run that had almost killed him. He'd wanted to believe she was guilty. That would have made his life a lot easier, but he'd sensed the truth in her words and had known she was a dead-end lead.

He'd keep digging, just in case. Ask Mrs. Smithfield a few questions. Get some facts to go with his gut instinct, but at the end of the day, he'd end up right back where he'd started. Nowhere. He had to try anyway. Mrs. Smithfield was loyal enough to Morgan that she wouldn't spread rumors. Hopefully she'd be willing to talk about the gallery owner if what she had to say didn't seem harmful.

"Morgan has a beautiful gallery."

As he'd hoped, his companion was quick to nod her agreement. "Yes, doesn't she? This place was quite a wreck when she moved in, you know."

"No, I didn't."

"Nearly crumbling. The foundation had to be reinforced, termites had to be eradicated. Not to mention the mice and roaches." She shuddered delicately, her white curls shaking in response.

"I guess it cost a good amount of money to have all that work done."

"I suppose so, though I'm much too polite to ask." Her faded brown eyes flashed with disapproval as she opened the back door of a red Crown Victoria.

"Of course you are." He should have known he was heading in the wrong direction with his questions. Too much time away from his job. His interrogation skills were rusty.

"I do know it cost a lot in time, though. Morgan arrived in town two months before the shop opened." She took the bag of pottery from his hands and set it on the car floor.

"She's been in Lakeview for four months?" That would put her move at just a few weeks after her husband's conviction, long before the hit-and-run.

"Thereabouts. She rented a room above my garage until this place was ready. That's how we met. She called asking about my ad. Such a sweet young lady, and she seemed so downtrodden and sad."

"She's had a tough time."

"Yes, she has. That no-good husband of hers…" She smiled and shook her head. "But I'm saying more than I have a right to. I'm sure if you know Morgan, you know what she's been through."

"Some of it."

"Well, what you don't know, you'll have to find out from her. Thank you again for walking me to the car."

"It was no problem."

"Now, go back in there and buy something pretty for your wife."

"My mother."

"Her, too, but, really, it was obvious your wife loved the gallery. I'm sure buying her something would put you in her good graces for a long time to come."

"Lacey isn't—"

"It has to be something beautiful. Maybe a gorgeous vase that can be filled with flowers. My husband used to buy me flowers every Monday. I'd put them in a vase, set them on the kitchen table and look at them every time the kids got too out of hand or the endless chores seemed too monotonous to bear. I would be reminded of the first time I looked into my husband's eyes, how I was so sure I could see forever. It made all the monotony and chores and endless scraping and saving just to make ends meet worthwhile."

Surprised, Jude studied Mrs. Smithfield's face. It was lined with age and with laughter and held the kind of beauty that was gained by a life lived well. "My father used to say that."

"What?" She smiled vaguely, her focus still on the past and all its memories.

"That when he looked into my mother's eyes, he'd seen forever."

"Yes, well, that is how all the great love stories begin." She smiled more broadly, her eyes focusing on Jude once again. "My husband is gone now. Been gone for seven years, but I still miss him. Every Monday, I look at the empty kitchen table and I think about the day we met and the day we'll meet again." There were tears in her eyes, and Jude patted her shoulder, wishing he were better at offering comfort. In some ways his job had hardened him, made him immune to tears and sadness. In others, it had softened him, serving as a constant reminder that life was finite. That loved ones wouldn't always be around.

"I'm sure your husband is still thinking of you, too. Anticipating the moment he'll see you again."

"Oh, I'm sure Ladd is too busy exploring Heaven to think much about me." She sniffed and straightened her shoulders. "But that's more than enough of that foolishness. It's too beautiful a day to be teary-eyed."

"It is that, Mrs. Smithfield." He held her elbow as she lowered herself into the car.

"Thank you, young man. Now, go on back inside. I'm sure that lovely wife of yours is wondering where you've gotten to." She closed the door and drove away, her words still ringing in his ears.

I was so sure I could see forever.

Her words.

His father's words.

A silly notion that he had no business dwelling on.

He frowned and walked back to the shop, determined to push the words out of his head. He didn't have time to think about them, or to wonder what he'd seen gleaming so faintly in Lacey's eyes.

It hadn't been forever. That was for sure.

"Jude? I think I found something perfect for your mom." Lacey's appeared in the doorway of the shop, her eyes filled with mysteries that begged exploration.

"A red rooster teapot?" He smiled, caught in her gaze, the beauty he found there.

"It's much cooler than that. See?" She lifted a delicate blue teapot, its handle a fragile braid intertwined with pale-yellow flowers. It looked like something his mother would enjoy. Decorative and frivolous. The kind of thing she'd never have owned when she'd had four rambunctious boys and a terror of a daughter running around the house.

"You're right. My mother would love that."

"It's expensive." She smiled apologetically as she handed it to him.

"I'm sure Detective Sinclair doesn't mind spending a little extra on the woman who raised him." Morgan smiled sweetly as Jude turned to face her, but the sharp interest in her gaze was unmistakable. Obviously, she was as interested in finding out why he'd come to call as he had been in finding out why she'd moved to Lakeview. He didn't plan to fill her in. Hopefully Lacey hadn't, either. The fewer people who knew that Jude was on the hunt, the easier it would be to surprise his prey.

"You're right. I don't mind. My mother is into these kinds of things."

"What kind would that be?" Lacey asked as Morgan carefully wrapped the teapot and placed it in a bag.

"Delicate and girlie."

"There's nothing wrong with delicate and girlie, you know."

Especially not when it looks like you.

The flattery almost slipped out, but Jude managed to seal his lips before it did. Good thing. Flattery led to other things. Things he wasn't prepared for. Like expectation, commitment, relationship. None of those were on his agenda. "You're right. There's not. Delicate and girlie just are not very practical."

"That teapot has a practical use. It's going to make your mother happy."

"There's that." Jude paid and walked outside, Lacey close on his heels.

"Morgan seems nice."

"I guess she does."

"You sound disappointed."

"I am. I want an end to this."

"Maybe…" Her voice trailed off, but Jude knew what she was going to say. He'd said the same to himself every day for two months. Maybe it already *was* over. Maybe the feeling that he was being hunted was all in his head.

"I want to believe it's over, Lacey. That what happened in New York was the end. But I don't. And I've got to go with my instincts on this one. If I don't, I might pay with my life."

"I understand."

"Do you?" He pulled open the car door, waiting as she got inside.

"I know what it feels like to have danger breathing down my neck and to know that at any minute it might pounce. And I know what it feels like to face it alone."

"Is that what happened here?" He lifted her wrist, brushing back the thick coat she wore, and ran his finger along one of the scars.

"Don't." She jerked back, turning away and hugging her arms tight to her waist.

"Someone hurt you."

"A lifetime ago. It's not something I think about anymore."

"I don't believe you."

"You don't have to. Will you move so I can close the door? It's freezing out."

He hesitated, then did as she asked. Pressuring her to reveal what had happened would only hurt her more than she already had been.

She was shivering when he got in the car, and he took off his jacket, leaning over to tuck it around her legs.

"*I'm* supposed to be taking care of *you*. Not the other way around." She started to tug the jacket off, but Jude stilled her hands.

"Take it until the car warms up."

"I'm not a victim anymore, Jude. I don't need a police officer to cover me with his coat and protect me from the ugliness that has already happened."

Her words were more telling than she probably realized. Jude clenched his fists, his stomach churning with anger. "I'm protecting you from the cold, Lacey. That's all."

She frowned, her eyes filled with a million secrets. Jude knew he could stare into them forever and never find everything there was to see.

Forever?

He shoved the keys in the ignition and started the car. Dreams of forever were for people who wanted to be tied down. Men and women who were like his parents, his brothers Grayson and Tristan and his sister Piper. They weren't for Jude. At least they'd never been before. He'd wanted independence and freedom, and he'd gotten it when he'd moved to New York. He'd been happy with it. At least for the first few years.

Lately, his New York apartment and bachelor life had seemed empty. He'd started wondering if independence and freedom cost a lot more than he was willing to pay.

He pushed the thoughts to the back of his mind.

This wasn't the time to be thinking about long-ago choices any more than it was the time to be staring into Lacey's eyes. Jude had a killer to find. Until he did that, there was no sense thinking about the past or worrying about the future.

"Look, there's a sign for Booker T. Washington National Monument. We can go for that walk." Lacey sounded like she'd just won the lottery, and Jude didn't have the heart to tell her he had more important things to do than stroll through the woods.

"Weren't you just complaining about how cold it is outside?"

"I'll warm up once we're moving. I've been reading about the plantation where Booker T. Washington grew up. It would be fun to see it. My last client wasn't well enough to do much more than sit in the house. I spent nine months longing for the outdoors."

"You don't get days off during the week?"

"Sure. Two. Like everyone else. I just don't always take them."

"What days do you get off working for me?"

"Monday and Sunday afternoon."

"Not the whole day on Sunday?"

"Grayson wanted to make sure you always had a ride to church. Since I planned on attending, I didn't mind agreeing to working Sunday morning."

"Then I guess we owe you another half day off."

"I won't need it. I like to keep busy. Especially if it involves outings like this." She smiled as he took the exit that led to the monument.

"In that case, we'll have to take more of them. Maybe I can get my hands on a canoe and take you exploring the lake." The offer popped out of Jude's mouth before he thought it through. He liked Lacey. She was quick-witted and funny. Strong and resilient. Spending time out on the lake with her wouldn't be a hardship. The more he thought about it, the better he liked the idea. Too bad life was so complicated. Too bad keeping Lacey close might put her in danger.

"I don't think that would be such a good idea. Riding in a canoe with you would feel too much like…" She blushed and grabbed the door handle.

Jude stopped her before she could get out of the car. "Like what? A date?"

"Yes."

"Would that be so bad?"

"Yes! You're a client."

"I won't always be."

"That's not the point." She sounded so appalled, Jude let the subject drop. Now wasn't the time to pursue it.

Eventually Jude would take Lacey out in a canoe, show her the austere beauty of the lake in the winter.

If he survived long enough.

The thought was an unwelcome intrusion, but one Jude couldn't ignore. The clock was ticking, and somewhere a murderer waited to strike again.

TEN

Lacey scrambled out of the car, hoping the fresh air would knock some sense into her.

Alone with Jude in a canoe?

She'd said no to the suggestion, but her mind had been screaming, *Yes! Yes! A thousand times, yes!*

Obviously, picking out a gift for Jude's mother had rattled her brain, reminding Lacey of a time when she hadn't understood what real love was. Then, she would have done anything to earn her mother's or stepfather's love. She hadn't realized that neither of them were capable of more than they were already giving. It had taken half a dozen years to learn her lesson, but once she had, Lacey had given up her good-girl persona and embraced her inner rebel. It had gotten her into a world of trouble, but at least it had gotten her something.

And almost cost her everything.

She winced away from the thought, hurrying toward a dirt path at the edge of the parking lot.

"We in a hurry?" Jude got out of the car, his question stopping Lacey's frantic retreat.

"No. Of course not." She stood still, despite the frantic urge to run. Away from her memories. Away from Jude and his intense gaze.

"Good, because I don't do hurry very well anymore." He popped the trunk of his Mustang and pulled out a backpack. "I've got a couple of bottles of water in here and some protein bars. That should keep us going for a while."

"I'll carry it." She moved toward Jude. The cold, crisp air bathed her cheeks and stung her eyes. The silence of the morning, the beauty of the winter brown fields and the evergreen trees, reminded her that the past was only that.

"I hope that was a joke."

"Why would it be?"

"Because I can manage my own pack. Here." He held out his jacket. "Put this on over your coat."

"And let you freeze? I don't think so."

"I've got a fleece pullover in the pack. I'll wear that." He unzipped the backpack and pulled out a gray pullover.

"I'll wear that and you can wear your coat." Lacey tugged the sweatshirt from his hands and slipped out of her coat. It took only seconds to pull on the oversize fleece, but she was already shivering when she put her coat back on.

"You've got thin blood, Lacey. Better button up." Jude took a step closer, the clean, masculine scent of him mixing with pine needles and outdoors. Before Lacey realized what he was doing, he'd buttoned the top button of her coat, his knuckles brushing against her chin, the feel of them spearing through her. She wanted to back up and step out of reach, turn toward the building that beckoned in the distance, but his touch held her captive. The warmth of his fingers as he reached around and pulled strands of hair from the collar of her coat made Lacey wonder why she'd avoided men for so long.

Because they hurt you. That's why. They chew you up and spit you out. And sometimes they do even worse.

Better keep that in mind, little girl. Because a kid like you is sure to attract plenty of boys. All the wrong kind.

Her stepfather's words filled her head, his warning drifting through time and distance. She hadn't listened then, but she'd learned the hard way that the man she'd despised had been right. She did attract the wrong kind of boys. The wrong kind of men.

She shifted away, putting distance between herself and Jude the way she should have the second he'd touched her. "I can manage the rest, thanks."

She had mittens in her pocket. Colorful ones that had been knit by an elderly woman she'd cared for several years ago. Each stitch was made with love and a prayer. Or so Lacey had been told when she'd received them as a Christmas gift.

"Nice mittens." Jude smiled as she pulled them on, and she couldn't blame him for being amused. Poor Mrs. Jennings had been nearly blind, and her color choices had reflected it. Bright pink, neon orange and sapphire blue were liberally mixed with deep purple and fuchsia.

"They are, aren't they?"

"I've never seen anything like them. Did you make them yourself?" He hooked her arm with his and started walking toward one of the distant buildings.

"They were a gift from one of my clients."

"She was quite an artisan." The words might have been mocking or sincere, and Lacey shot a quick look in Jude's direction, trying to read his expression.

"If you're being sarcastic—"

"I'm not. I appreciate anything handcrafted. I don't have the patience to do anything intricate or artistic, and I admire people who do. Those mittens probably took hours to make."

"Longer than that for Mrs. Jennings. She was nearly blind and had arthritis in both hands."

"That makes the mittens extra special, then."

"I've always thought so."

They stepped up in front of the brick building, and Jude frowned. "Looks like the monument is closed for the winter."

"Too bad. I was really looking forward to exploring."

"We still can. There's a path through the woods. I don't see any harm in taking it."

"But—"

"Come on, Lacey, be adventurous." He walked away, the slight hitch in his stride a reminder of why they were there. Jude needed to be out walking and exercising, rebuilding his strength so he could regain his independence.

"I *am* adventurous."

"Then let's go." He stopped and looked over his shoulder, sunlight playing across his hard features and glinting in his eyes as he waited, making him look even more handsome.

Who was Lacey kidding?

He couldn't get any more handsome.

Which wouldn't have been so bad if he hadn't also been nice.

Why couldn't he have been ugly and mean, or arrogant and rude? Why did he have to be handsome and kind and just a little bit sweet?

She sighed, hurrying up beside him, her heart skipping a beat as he smiled. "I knew you had it in you. Now if I get arrested, I won't be alone."

"You think we're going to get arrested?" That would be hard to explain to her supervisor. *Sorry, James. I can't work for a few years. I got caught trespassing on government land and I'm in jail. Oh, and before I forget, I got my client arrested, too.*

"No, but if you keep scowling like that, I might be tempted to throw you in jail."

"I'm not scowling."

"Sure you are." He laughed softly and took her hand, pulling her along a path lined with thick foliage.

"You're a pain in the neck. You know that, Jude?"

"I've been told it a time or two. But I don't think that's the real reason you're frowning."

"You're right. It's not. I'm frowning because I'm trying to figure out how I'm going to explain to my supervisor that I got the two of us thrown into jail."

He laughed again, brushing strands of hair from her cheek, his fingers lingering. "I really don't think that's going to happen."

"Good, because I can't afford to lose my job."

"You know, you've really surprised me, Lacey."

"Why do you say that?" she asked, even though she wasn't sure she wanted to know. Wasn't sure she wanted a man like Jude to be surprised by her. That might lead him to ask more questions she wouldn't answer. Couldn't answer.

"When I met you, I thought you were the kind of woman who considered high tea an adventure. The kind who'd be content to sit back and watch the world go by. Obviously, you're not."

"You're right. I'm not."

"The thing is, now that I know who you're not, I want to know who you are."

"You already know who I am. Lacey Carmichael, home-care aide."

"That's what you do. It isn't who you are."

"You're wrong. It's exactly who I am. Come on. We were going for a walk. Remember?"

"You're changing the subject. I guess I'm making you uncomfortable."

"Your brother hired me to do a job, Jude. Who I am, what I think and feel, are really none of your business."

"I keep telling myself that, but I'm not listening."

"You should be. In a month, you'll be back to your old self and I'll be at a new job with a new client. We'll both move on with our lives and forget the other person even exists."

"You think so?"

No.

"Of course."

"So you won't be telling stories about me the way you do about Mrs. Jennings?

"Only if you knit me colorful mittens."

He laughed, the sound ringing out through the woods, nearly hiding the sound of something crashing through the underbrush.

Something or someone.

A blur of movement. A figure racing out onto the path. Featureless. Terrifying. Lacey screamed, felt something slam into her. Jude. Shoving her back the way they'd come, shouting for her to run.

She ran several yards back up the path, her heart beating so hard and so loud she could hear nothing else. Not her panting breath. Not her feet slamming against the ground. Not Jude running beside her.

Jude.

She skidded to a stop, turning, seeing him on the ground, struggling. Fighting. Winning.

Or losing.

She couldn't tell which and couldn't leave him there to fight alone.

She raced back, fishing in her pocket and pulling out her cell phone. She dialed quickly, shouting their location to the 9-1-1 operator.

Something flashed in the sunlight. A knife.

Lacey's heart nearly stopped, the phone dropping from her hand as she lunged forward and grabbed the blade before it plunged into Jude's throat.

Blood spurted from her palm and slid down her wrist, but she held on as Jude rolled to the side.

"Lacey! Go!" He shouted the command as he pulled a gun.

She tried, but something snagged her shirt. Pulled her in. The blade of the knife pressed against her neck and she froze.

"Drop the gun." The hissed command barely registered above Lacey's throbbing terror, but Jude must have heard. He dropped the gun, kicking it into the undergrowth, his eyes boring into Lacey's.

What was he trying to tell her?

Did he want her to fight?

Or did he want her hold still and wait for him to do something?

If that was the case, she hoped he would do something soon, because she didn't think her legs were going to hold her much longer.

"Move." Lacey was shoved forward, the knife still at her throat. She did what she was told, shuffling toward the undergrowth where Jude had thrown the gun.

Please, Lord, don't let this guy get his hands on the gun. Please, keep Jude and me safe.

The prayer raced through her mind as the sound of sirens filled the air.

Lacey's captor cursed under his breath and shoved her forward. She stumbled, landing on her hands and knees, her breath leaving on a gasp of pain.

"Hold it right there." Jude shouted the command, and Lacey wasn't sure if it was directed at her or at their attacker.

There was a thud. Another curse.

The knife clattered onto the ground, and Lacey grabbed it, scrambling to her feet, searching for Jude. He was dragging their attacker up, reaching for his ski mask. The man pulled back, slamming his foot into Jude's thigh.

Jude dropped like a rock, and Lacey raced forward, the knife still in her hand. She thought the masked man would turn on her, maybe try to take the knife or find the gun. Instead, he turned on his heels and ran into the woods, moving so fast it took a moment for Lacey to realize he was gone.

Jude jumped up and gave chase, his limp slowing him as he crashed through the underbrush and disappeared from view, leaving Lacey alone. The sunlight filtered through the trees and washed the world in gold, hiding the violence that had been there.

ELEVEN

Fury masked Jude's pain as he raced through thick undergrowth and shoved his way through heavy brush. Up ahead, he could hear the crack of branches and a mumbled curse. He was close to his attacker. If his bum legs worked a little better, he'd have caught the guy by now. The thought only added fuel to his rage and made him even more determined to catch their attacker.

Their attacker.

Not just his.

An image of Lacey's hand closing over the blade of the knife flashed through his mind. Blood spurting from colorful knit. He wanted to ignore it and keep single-mindedly racing toward his goal, but as much as the need to stop the masked knifeman pulled him forward, Lacey pulled him back.

He slowed his pace, scowling as he turned back the way he'd come. He couldn't leave her bleeding and alone.

"I don't suppose You want to send some help, God?" He muttered the prayer aloud, knowing God wasn't going to answer. Why should He? Jude had spent as little time thinking about God as he could during the past years. Sure, he believed, but belief didn't mean relationship.

It had only been lately that he'd thought that through and

realized just how empty his soul was. Work, friends, adventures: they weren't enough to fill the barren darkness inside.

The sound of breaking branches came from somewhere in front and to the left of him, and Jude froze.

Listening. Waiting. Their attacker returning?

He didn't think so.

There was no way the guy could have moved fast enough to circle back. Sirens blared somewhere close by. Maybe the cavalry had arrived. Or maybe Lacey had.

He strode forward, catching sight of her pale-blond hair seconds before the scent of rain and flowers filled his nose. "Lacey?"

She screamed, stopping so suddenly she almost fell backward, the knife clenched in her uninjured hand. "You nearly scared me to death."

"Good. Maybe next time when I tell you to run, you'll do it."

"I did run."

"Yeah, but you didn't keep going." He sounded harsher than he intended, and he tried to soften his voice. "You could have been killed, Lacey."

"You could have been, too."

"That's not the point." He shrugged out of his coat, pulled off his T-shirt and pressed it against Lacey's bleeding palm.

"Then what is? If I'd lived and you'd died, would that have made it better?"

He didn't have anything to say to that, so he kept silent, pressing against the wound that still seeped blood, grinding his teeth to keep from lecturing Lacey like he wanted to.

"Has it stopped bleeding?" She tried to pull away, but Jude held firm.

"It's deep. You're going to need stitches."

"I doubt it. It barely hurts." She tugged again, and this time he let her pull away, watched as she peeled back the T-shirt and looked at the deep slash.

"It's not so bad."

"How about we let a doctor decide?" He took the knife she still held and slid his arm around her back, walking her toward the parking lot. Her body trembled, but her breathing was steady, her pace unrushed. She was good under pressure. Better than some cops he'd worked with.

Voices echoed through the trees. The cavalry riding to the rescue too late to do any good. No way would the perpetrator hang around and wait to be caught. The thought only added to Jude's frustration. He wanted to head back into the woods, chase their attacker down. He'd been so close to seeing the guy's face. A split second. That was all Jude would have needed. Instead, he'd gotten a swift kick to his left thigh. His bad thigh.

He didn't think that was an accident. Whoever had attacked them knew where Jude was weakest.

How?

Who?

More questions without answers.

More reason for frustration.

An officer appeared on the path in front of them. Young. Green. His hand hovering over the butt of his gun. "Drop the knife, buddy."

Jude did what he was told, tossing the weapon onto the ground and frowning at the sight of Lacey's blood smeared on the blade.

"Good. Now just stay where you are until we figure out exactly what's going on here."

"Look, we're the victims here. The guy who attacked us is heading southwest through the woods." Jude took a step forward.

"I said stay where you are." The officer didn't pull his gun, but Jude could see he was itching to.

Jude stopped, positioning himself between the gung-ho cop and Lacey. "My friend is hurt. I need to take her to the emergency room."

"I'll make sure she gets there."

"Yeah. And while you do, the guy who cut her is getting away."

"Like I said, we'll get everything figured out. Ma'am? You want to come over here with me?"

Jude gritted his teeth and kept his mouth shut as Lacey peered out from behind him. "Actually, I'm fine where I am."

"Can you tell me who hurt you?"

"I didn't see his face."

"So it wasn't the gentleman you're with?"

"Of course it wasn't him." She took a step out from behind him, and Jude put a hand on her arm to hold her in place. He wanted to get her out of the woods and to a hospital. He wanted to take her home, wrap her in warm blankets and give her a steaming cup of hot cocoa. He did not want to stand around playing nice with a greenhorn cop who didn't know a criminal from a victim.

"Let's sit in my cruiser to discuss it. It's warmer there." Separate the feuding parties. It was the typical MO for dealing with domestic-violence cases and exactly what Jude would have done in the same situation, but time was wasting and a knife-wielding killer was getting farther away.

"Look, this isn't a case of domestic violence. My friend and I were out for a walk and—"

"Everything under control here?" Another officer jogged toward them. Older and probably more experienced, but staring at Jude like he was a roach in need of a good stomping.

"We've got one injury. Lady's hand is bleeding pretty badly. She needs transport to the E.R. She and her friend say a third party attacked her." *But I don't believe either of them. I think the guy is scum and can't control his temper. I think he attacked his girl, and she's afraid to say so.*

Jude could almost hear the unspoken words.

"We told you that because that's what happened." Lacey sounded as frustrated as Jude felt, and he squeezed her hand.

"We'll get it all sorted out, ma'am. Why don't you go with Officer Reynolds while I talk to your friend?"

"I'd rather stay here."

"You need to get to the hospital. Your friend will join you there as soon he can." The older police officer eyed Jude while he spoke. "That okay with you, buddy?"

As if Jude actually had a say in it.

He nodded anyway, anxious to move things along. Get back to the hunt and find the guy who'd hurt Lacey. Who would have done a lot worse if he'd had a chance. "It's fine by me. Listen, I'm a New York City homicide detective. My badge is in my back pocket. The guy who attacked my friend and me is heading through the woods. If we don't go after him now, we're not going to find him."

"One thing at a time. Reynolds, you want to take the lady back to the cars? Call an ambulance to transport her to the hospital. We can get her statement there."

"Really, I don't think I need—"

But Officer Reynolds put a hand on Lacey's shoulder and urged her away before she could finish the thought. She glanced back at Jude as she went, her eyes filled with fear. She looked fragile and scared and so lonely that Jude took a step toward her.

"How about you stay here, Detective…?"

"Sinclair. Jude."

"Sinclair?"

"That's right." The conversation barely registered. Jude was too busy watching Lacey walk away.

"You got any brothers?"

"Several."

"Any from around here?"

"Grayson and Tristan."

"Grayson Sinclair the district attorney?"

"That's right." *Now, can we get back to the problem at hand?* Jude bit back the sarcastic question.

"And you're the brother that nearly had his legs sev—" The officer's voice trailed off.

"Severed. That would be me."

"I'm Blake McKnight." He held out a hand, gave Jude's a firm shake. "Want to tell me what happened here today?"

"My friend and I were hiking. Some guy charged out of the woods and attacked."

"You see his face?"

"He was wearing a mask."

"Height and weight?"

"Six one. Maybe two-twenty."

"A big guy. Any idea of skin color?"

"He was wearing gloves, long pants and a coat. I didn't see any skin."

"It happened here?"

"Farther down the trail. My service revolver is there, too."

"You fired it?"

"No."

"I'm going to call in a CSI unit. They'll collect the evidence. Then you and I will go for a walk, see what we can find. Could be the guy left enough tracks for us to follow."

"The way he was running, I'm sure he did." And Jude was anxious to go on the hunt. Searching through the woods for signs a killer had been there beat waiting around for him to strike again. But searching also meant leaving Lacey. She and Officer Reynolds rounded a curve in the path and disappeared from view, and Jude frowned.

"What hospital will my friend be transported to?"

"Lakeview General. Officer Reynolds will make sure she's okay."

"I'm sure he will, but it might be good if I was there, too.

Lacey is new to town. She might feel more comfortable having someone she knows nearby."

"You two are dating?" Officer McKnight asked casually, as he used gloved hands to pick up the knife. "Thing is sharp. The guy who attacked you meant business. Did he try to steal anything? Maybe pull off your backpack? Grab your friend's purse?"

"We're not dating. And Lacey wasn't carrying a purse. The guy didn't go for anything but my throat."

"Someone has something out for you?" McKnight glanced up from the bag he was placing the knife in.

"More than one person, but I think this might be connected to the hit-and-run in New York."

"That was what? Three months ago?"

"Two."

"Seems like someone who wanted you dead wouldn't have waited two months to finish the job."

"I was in the hospital for almost a month and spent a week in rehab before I came to Lynchburg. He might not have had an opportunity." Jude led Officer McKnight to the undergrowth where he'd kicked the gun. "My service revolver is here. The perp never touched it. Mind if I take it with me?"

"It's evidence."

"It's also protection. I think you'll agree that I need it." He lifted it and shoved it into his holster, antsy, irritated and ready to go. Not after the perpetrator but after Lacey.

"Today could have been a random crime, Sinclair."

"It could have been, but I don't think it was." He quickly filled Officer McKnight in on the previous night's events.

McKnight glanced up from the pad he was writing in. "You know I still want to think it's random, right?"

"It's not what you want to think that matters." Jude started back the way they'd come.

"I think you've been a cop for a long time, and I think if you say someone is after you, I've got no choice but to check it out."

"Thanks."

"I also think I need you here helping with the investigation, so wherever you're going will have to wait."

"Sorry, I need to be with my friend."

"The one who isn't your girlfriend?" He smirked, and Jude had the urge to wipe it off his face.

"Lacey was hired to work as a home-care aide during my recovery. She wouldn't be here—and wouldn't be injured—if it wasn't for me. I need to make sure she's okay."

"I get that you're concerned about her, but you need to be just as concerned about you. The sooner we figure out who attacked you, the better."

"I can't leave Lacey alone at the hospital, so whatever you're going to do to find the guy you'll have to do without me." He continued walking, stopping when McKnight dropped a hand on his shoulder.

"I need your input, Sinclair, and the longer it takes to get it, the less likely it will be that we'll find the person responsible. It's not just you who is in danger. Lacey is, too. She's the one in the hospital right now. It might be worse the next time."

And there would be a next time.

There was no doubt about that.

Jude hesitated, torn between leaving and staying. For now, Lacey was fine, but McKnight was right. If they didn't find the person responsible for the attack, she might not stay that way. "Let me call some people. See if I can get someone to go to the hospital with her."

"Good call, friend."

It was. Jude knew it, but even as he pulled out his cell phone and dialed, his mind was filled with Lacey. The blood staining her mitten, her hair falling in disarray, her eyes filled with fear.

And for the first time in more years than he cared to admit, he prayed for someone else. His plea lifting up to a God he'd ignored for much too long. A God who had tugged and pulled at Jude's heart from the time he was old enough to know what salvation meant. A God who held the present and the future in His hand.

A God, Jude realized, he couldn't ignore any longer.

TWELVE

Lacey hated hospitals; hated the scent of illness and grief that lingered beneath antiseptic and bleach. Hated the sterile atmosphere and the hushed anticipation that filled the air. More than any of those things, she hated the memories that being in hospitals always brought.

Pain. Terror. Betrayal. Loneliness. The sudden, clear understanding that life as she knew it had ended.

Her heart raced with all those things as she settled onto a gurney and waited. The small triage room was as sterile as any hospital's, the walls painted beige, the floor tiled. There was no clock, of course. More than likely Lacey would sit there alone for hours, waiting for someone to come in and look at the cut on her hand.

She glanced at it, frowning. Her mitten was gone, thanks to the paramedics who'd treated her at the scene, and the cut was covered by thick gauze that was already stained with blood.

Good thing she wasn't squeamish.

Lacey picked at the tape, lifted the edge of the gauze and frowned again. Another scar to add to the rest. At least she was alive. Jude was alive. Those were both things to thank God for and to concentrate on while she waited in her sterile little prison for the doctor to arrive and inflict massive quantities of pain.

"Way to be positive, Lacey." She grumbled and stood, then paced across the room, peering out into the hallway.

She could make a run for it. With or without stitches, her hand would eventually heal.

Then again, she didn't have a car and she didn't have any money. At least she didn't think she did. She dug in her pocket, found a dollar fifty in change and a few pieces of colored lint. Not enough for cab fare, but it would get her a chocolate bar if she could find a vending machine.

"Lacey Carmichael?" A dark-haired woman hurried toward her. Five-five. Late fifties. Slim, attractive, well put together. Not dressed in a nurse's uniform or wearing a stethoscope. That had to be a good thing.

"Yes."

"I thought so. You look just like Jude described, but since you were coming out of the room the nurse said you were waiting in, I wasn't sure." She smiled, her eyes deep-blue and vaguely familiar.

"You're a friend of Jude's?"

"Of sorts. I'm his mother." She smiled again, and Lacey suddenly knew why her eyes looked familiar. Aside from the color, they were just like Jude's. The same shape. The same amusement dancing in them.

"His mother?" She sounded like a parrot repeating every word, but Lacey's brain didn't seem to be functioning well.

Had Jude sent his mother to make sure she was okay?

The thought was disconcerting.

And touching.

"Yes. He's been held up at the crime scene." Her gaze dropped to Lacey's hand, and she shook her head. "Such a terrible thing. I can't believe you were attacked so brutally."

"It was terrifying, but Jude and I are both okay. I guess that's all that matters."

"It is, and I think we should all be thanking God for your safety. Things could have been much worse. So, tell me, were you heading anywhere in particular?" She raised a dark eyebrow, smiling again.

"The nearest vending machine. I need a chocolate fix."

"Then I'm just in time. Come back in the room. I've got some chocolate bars in my purse."

Chocolate was great. Escape would be better. "Actually, I was also thinking about grabbing a cab and heading back to the duplex."

"A grand escape?"

"I'm not sure how grand it would have been, but that was the plan."

"I'd offer you a ride, but Jude asked me to make sure you got the treatment you needed. I wouldn't be any kind of mother if I let him down." She smiled sweetly, but Lacey suspected there was a will of steel behind her charm.

Obviously, Jude had come by his strong personality naturally. "I guess I'll settle for the chocolate, then."

She followed Mrs. Sinclair back into the triage room, wrinkling her nose as the antiseptic smell enveloped her again. "I've never liked hospitals."

The confession slipped out, and Jude's mother nodded sympathetically. "Me, neither. Unfortunately, with five very active kids in the house, I've spent more than my fair share of time in them. Jude's broken bones alone had us in the emergency room five times. That's not counting wounds that needed stitching, poked eyes." She sighed and dug into her purse, pulling out two chocolate bars and handing one to Lacey.

"Thank you, Mrs. Sinclair."

"Becca. That's what my friends call me, and I'm sure after a few hours bonding in this room, that's what we'll be."

"I guess so. I'm sorry Jude asked you to come here. I was

really fine by myself." Although she couldn't help being glad for the company and for the distraction it offered.

"Don't be. I could have said no if I'd wanted to. Is there anyone you want me to call? Family? Friends?"

"No. Thank you, though." Even if Lacey's mother lived locally, there was no way she would bother coming to sit by Lacey's side. Which seemed even sadder than usual, considering the fact that Jude's mother, a total stranger, had dropped everything to be there.

"Jude said you don't have family around. Are they far from here?"

"Yes."

"That must be hard, being so far from people who love you." Becca's eyes were filled with compassion, and there was no way Lacey planned to tell her the truth. That there was no one who came even close to loving her the way she'd always dreamed a family should.

"I'm used to it. I've been working as a home-care aide for ten years. Traveling is part of the job."

"You must meet a lot of interesting people."

"I do. That's one of the best parts of the job."

"And what do you do when you're not working? Explore new places? Get involved in community activities? Attend church?"

Uh-oh. Lacey knew where this was going, and she didn't like it. Becca was feeling her out, trying to see if Lacey was good enough for her son.

A petite, dark-haired woman appeared in the doorway, saving Lacey from having to respond. "Becca Sinclair, please tell me you're not interrogating an injured woman."

"*Interrogating* is such a harsh word, Honor. I prefer to think of it as showing interest in her life." Becca smiled sheepishly, but the twinkle in her eyes said she wasn't at all sorry.

"Whatever you want to call it, you should be ashamed of yourself." There was a hint of Irish brogue in Honor's voice and a warmth in her eyes that belied the sternness of her tone. "You'll have to excuse Becca," she said to Lacey. "She is very protective of her family."

"As are you." Becca smiled and hugged Honor. "I take it my son asked you to come here, too."

"Asked? Demand is more what Jude did." She smiled at Lacey. "I'm Honor Malone."

"Lacey Carmichael."

"Jude said you'd been injured. A knife wound?"

"It's nothing serious."

"Well, I'll have to look at it, seeing as how Jude asked so nicely." She leaned over Lacey's bandaged hand and started unwrapping it.

"That's really not necessary, Honor. I'm sure the doctor will be in shortly."

"Probably, but I'm a nurse, and I promised Jude I'd take a look. I can't break my promise and get in bad with a future in-law." Her eyes widened, and she put a hand over her mouth. "That's supposed to be a secret until tomorrow."

"A secret? Why would you keep such wonderful news from me?" Becca jumped to her feet and wrapped Honor in another hug.

"Grayson was planning to tell you tomorrow when we stopped by after church. He'll be disappointed that I've spilled the beans without him."

"What he doesn't know won't hurt him. And what I know is going to keep me floating on air for a week." Becca beamed with excitement, and Honor laughed.

"I guess since I already slipped, I could show you some fabric I was looking at for linens for the reception. I've got a few swatches in my bag. Go ahead and get them out." She spoke as she turned back to Lacey and continued to unwrap the gauze bandage.

"Congratulations on your engagement. Grayson seemed like a great guy when I spoke to him."

"He is. One of the things I love most about him is that family is his top priority—but then, that's the way all the Sinclairs are."

Becca pulled scraps of fabric from Honor's bag. "Honor, these are absolutely stunning."

They were.

Pale peach, subtle lavender, sage-green.

The kind of colors Lacey might choose for her own wedding if she ever got married.

"Aren't they? Candace helped me pick them out."

"Your sister-in-law has wonderful taste. Have you chosen the colors for your bridal party?"

"Candace has. She's fallen in love with one of the dresses she saw in a bridal magazine. It's deep chocolate-brown. I hadn't the heart to say no. We'll do a sash in one of the linen colors. I think it will be lovely."

"What about Lily? How does she feel about a brown dress? I'm sure your little one has a strong opinion about it."

"Little one?" Surprised, Lacey met Honor's gaze.

"I have a four-year-old daughter from a previous marriage. My husband was killed in Iraq several years ago."

"I'm sorry for your loss."

"I am, too, but God put Grayson in my life, and I couldn't feel more blessed. Sometimes our deepest sorrow leads to our greatest joy."

"You've got such a wonderful attitude, Honor, and I feel blessed to have you as part of my family. I couldn't ask for a more wonderful daughter-in-law." Becca patted Honor's shoulder, a half smile on her face.

She looked gentle and sweet, the kind of woman anyone would be fortunate to have as a mother. The kind of woman Lacey had wished her mother was when she'd been a kid and still young enough to dream.

She was an adult now, but there were times when she still

longed for the connection she'd never had, still wished she could go back home, look in her mother's eyes and know she was loved.

"I see my mother and Honor are keeping you entertained while you wait." Jude's deep voice interrupted the quiet flow of words and pulled Lacey from her melancholy thoughts. Her pulse leaped, her heart jumping to attention, telling Lacey something she didn't want to hear but couldn't ignore.

She was attracted to Jude in a way she'd refused to allow herself to be attracted to anyone else in a very long time.

"It's a good thing, seeing as how long it took you to arrive." Becca smiled and placed a kiss on her son's cheek. "How are you, Jude?"

"Better." He wrapped her in a bear hug, kissed the top of her head and let her go. "Thanks for helping me out."

"You're my son. No thanks are necessary. Lacey is a wonderful young lady. As a matter of fact, I was just going to invite the two of you for lunch at our place tomorrow after church."

"Sorry, Mom. Grayson and Honor are stopping by after church tomorrow. We'll have to make it another day."

"Why not just all get together at the same time? I'll invite Piper and Caleb and Tristan and Martha. Honor, you can bring Lily and Candace. Unless that will interfere with your plans?"

"That would be perfect, Becca. I'll tell Grayson that we'll all meet at your place tomorrow."

"And you'll be there, Jude?"

Jude hesitated, then nodded. "Sure."

"Then it's settled. I'll see you all tomorrow after church. Lacey, it was wonderful to meet you. I only wish it had been under better circumstances." Becca took Lacey's hand and squeezed it gently. "If you need anything, please call. Now that all my children are grown, I've got way too much time on my hands."

"Mom, you're busier than most women I know who are half

your age." Jude walked his mother to the triage room entrance, waving as she walked away.

"I do like your mother, Jude. She's so sweet about getting her way." Honor laughed as she rewrapped Lacey's wound. "As for Lacey's hand, it still needs some stitching, but should heal just fine."

"Thanks for coming to take a look." He smiled, but his eyes were on Lacey.

"We're as good as family, so like your mother said, there's no need to thank me. Now, if you two will excuse me, I'd better get back home." Honor left the room and disappeared around the corner. Lacey and Jude found themselves alone in what had once been a decent-size room but now seemed too small.

"How's the hand?" He crossed the room and stood so close Lacey could smell the winter cold he'd brought in with him, fresh and clean and so much better than cleaners and bleach.

"Great. As a matter of fact, I've been thinking I'm not going to need stitches. Let's go." She scooted off the gurney and stood.

"I don't think so." He wrapped his hands around her waist and lifted her so effortlessly, Lacey wasn't even sure how it happened. One second she was standing. The next she was sitting again.

"Hey!"

"We're staying until the doctor comes."

"You could have just said so."

"I could have, but it wouldn't have been nearly as much fun." He grinned, but Lacey didn't miss his wince of pain or the way he shifted his weight from one foot to the other.

"Are you okay?" She touched his arm, felt the corded muscles beneath his shirt and pulled back, surprised at his strength and at her own visceral response to it.

"No worse than I've been before."

"Maybe the doctor—"

"How about we talk about something else?" His eyes flashed with irritation, and Lacey understood. Physical pain wasn't something that could be shared. Talking about it didn't make it go away, and it didn't make it better.

"I guess you managed to convince Officer McKnight that you weren't an abusive boyfriend."

"It didn't take long. Once my brother's name came up, McKnight got a whole lot more cooperative."

"Your brother?"

"Grayson is a district attorney."

"I didn't realize that."

"Fortunately for me, McKnight did. We started searching for our perp a few minutes after you left. By that time, it was already too late. He was long gone. And the only evidence he left behind was the knife."

"I'm sorry. I know you wanted this to be an end to your nightmare."

"I did, but I'm not giving up hope. He's out there, and he's getting impatient. That's going to be his downfall." His smile was tight and hard, and Lacey could imagine him confronting murderers, facing them down, pushing for confessions.

"What I don't understand is where he came from. We were alone. Then we weren't. I know he wasn't in the parking lot when we pulled in. It was empty."

"McKnight and I followed his tracks a quarter of a mile through the woods to the road we drove in on. We figure he had a car there, had probably followed us all morning, saw the opportunity and took it."

"That doesn't make me feel very safe." Lacey shivered, wishing she had the coat the police officer had taken from her before they'd gotten into the car. Evidence, he'd said. Lacey didn't know what kind he hoped to get. Human hair? Clothing fibers?

"It'll be okay." Jude eased down beside her, his hip pressed close to hers, his arm around her waist, pulling her in, offering comfort and expecting nothing in return. Lacey let herself relax into the moment, leaning her head against Jude's shoulder, letting their silence fill the room, fill *her* until she couldn't remember why she should keep her distance.

A quick rap on the door was like a splash of ice water in the face, and Lacey jumped off the gurney, her heart slamming in her chest, her mind screaming that she'd made a big mistake. Leaning on Jude? Allowing him to comfort her?

What had she been thinking?

Nothing. That's what.

"Ms. Carmichael?" A tall, austere-looking man entered the room, his white lab coat opened to reveal creased black slacks and a white dress shirt. He pushed a small cart with one hand, the gauze and needles on it giving Lacey a good idea of what she was in for.

"Yes?"

"I'm Dr. Gilliard. I hear you grabbed the wrong end of a hunting knife." His dark gaze dropped to her hand, then shifted to Jude who was leaning against the far wall. "Are you her husband?"

"I'm a friend."

"I see." Dr. Gilliard glanced at the chart he was holding. "Well, how about I take a look and see what we're dealing with. Have a seat, Ms. Carmichael." He gestured to the exam table, and Lacey forced herself to sit. What she really wanted to do was run. Not from the doctor, but from Jude.

He watched as the doctor unwrapped her hand and revealed the still seeping wound, his gaze steady and unwavering, his attention completely focused.

Lacey wanted to ask him to leave, but that would say something she'd rather not reveal—that Jude made her nervous, uncomfortable. Vulnerable.

"Wiggle your fingers for me."

Lacey did as the doctor asked, wiggling her fingers and opening and closing the hand, watching as blood seeped down her palm.

"Good. Looks like you're in luck, Ms. Carmichael. You missed serious damage by millimeters. We'll just get you stitched up and get you out of here."

"Want me to hold your hand?" Jude moved closer, reaching for her hand and holding it tight. Lacey could have told him there was no need. She wasn't afraid of needles or stitches or gaping, bleeding wounds. Sometimes she wasn't even sure she felt pain the same way other people did. A psychiatrist client she'd once worked for had told her that years of abuse could numb a person emotionally. What the psychiatrist hadn't seemed to know was that it could also numb them physically.

Lacey could have told Jude that, sent him away and let her hand lie cool and limp by her side as the doctor pushed the needle into her cut. Could have told him, but didn't. There was something too comforting about his touch, something too real and vital and wonderful.

She glanced his way, and he smiled, his eyes filled with compassion and concern and tinged with a touch of something deeper, more complicated. Lacey's heart jumped in acknowledgment.

Be careful, Lacey. Boys only want one thing. When they get it they'll push you out like yesterday's garbage and leave you to rot alone.

The voice whispered from the past, and Lacey shivered.

"It's okay. In another minute you won't feel a thing." Jude spoke close to her ear, his words warm as honey.

She wanted to tell him how wrong he was. That what she felt was a soul-deep pain that she could never quite get rid of. But the words stuck in her throat, and she just smiled and nodded and sat silently as the doctor finished stitching her wound.

It didn't take long, but by the time the doctor finished, Lacey felt as if she'd been sitting for hours. Her body was stiff, her mind numb, and for the first time in a long time, she wanted to do nothing more than sit in front of the television watching a mindless sitcom. A little comedy would cheer her glum mood. A mood that had more to do with Jude than she wanted to admit. Getting involved with him would be a mistake. A big one. He was a good guy. A great one. But relationships had never been Lacey's thing. She knew too much about how quickly they could go bad to ever want to take a chance with one again.

"You've gone quiet," Jude said as he took her hand and tugged her to her feet.

"Just thinking."

"About?"

"How quickly things change."

"Like?"

"Like one minute we're walking in the woods. The next, I'm sitting in the hospital." She dredged up a smile, took the release forms a nurse was handing her and pretended she wasn't scared to death of what she felt every time she looked into Jude's eyes.

"And now you're going home to get some rest. You look exhausted." Jude's fingers trailed down her cheek and came to rest on her jaw. He tilted her chin up, searching her face, seeing, she was sure, everything she felt. Everything she didn't want to feel.

"Jude, I don't think—"

"That this is a good idea? Me, neither, but I'm not sure there's anything either of us can do about it." He smiled gently, his hand falling away. "Come on, let's go home." He slipped his arm around her waist, led her out of the room and down the corridor. Away from the hospital. Toward home. A place Lacey hadn't known she'd been looking for, but that she suddenly thought she might have found. Not in a house, but in the arms of Jude Sinclair.

THIRTEEN

A good night's sleep did little to improve Lacey's mood. She frowned as she ran a brush through her hair and eyed her reflection in the mirror. Besides the thick bandage on her hand, she was no worse for wear. Her skin looked just a shade paler than it should have, but her hair fell straight over her shoulders and her eyes seemed a brighter green than usual. She'd chosen a simple turtleneck sweater dress that fell to her knees, the dove-gray color reminding her of Jude's gray pullover. Reminding her of Jude.

As if she needed a reminder.

He'd haunted her dreams, filled her thoughts. Made her wish her past was different, that she could believe in relationships and love the way other people did.

"But you don't, Lacey. Get it through your head. What works for other people will never work for you. No husband. No family. No house to go home to. It's you and God. And that's plenty." She scowled at her reflection as she spoke, smoothing her hair one last time before turning away. It was early to start the day, but she'd never been one to sit and wait. Keeping busy kept her from thinking about things she couldn't change.

She grabbed Jude's pullover, pulled on a wool coat and stepped outside.

Dawn had barely arrived and the world lay sleeping and still.

Deep purple and bright pinks painted the sky with color. Winter-dry grass rustled in the morning breeze. Tranquility and peace. Those were the things Lacey had been seeking for years. She'd never found them. There had been times when she'd come close, but here, in the shadow of Jude's porch, with the night just lifting, she felt she could stand forever, breathing in the silence, the peace, all the things she'd been searching for but had been sure she'd never find.

"You're up early again." Jude spoke quietly, his words a gentle caress that swept over her, pulled her in and under, made her want to believe in the dreams she'd given up on.

Fool.

You'll get hurt. And you'll deserve it.

She took a deep shuddering breath and turned to face Jude, schooling her features. Not wanting him to see how deeply he affected her. "So are you."

"Rough night." He limped toward her from the side of the house, his face drawn, his jaw tight.

"Is there anything I can do to help?"

"Just stand here with me for a few minutes. Make me forget that my legs don't work and my body wants to quit." He pressed in close, his shoulder touching hers, his scent surrounding them. Clean and strong.

But his physical weakness was obvious. His pain was something Lacey couldn't ignore. She slipped an arm around his waist, supporting him as she would any other client. But he wasn't any other client, and her pulse raced at the contact, her face heating. She refused to acknowledge either. The last thing Jude needed was for her to turn away because she was afraid to be close. He deserved better and needed more than that. "Do you want me to go get you some Tylenol?"

"I already told you what I want." He grumbled the reply, and Lacey frowned.

"I can stand here with you all day, but it won't take away the pain or make you forget."

"If you tell me a story it might."

"A story?"

"One about you."

"You're kidding."

"Do I look like I am?" He stared down into her eyes, and Lacey didn't see a hint of humor in his gaze.

"No, but that doesn't mean I'm going to tell you a story about my life."

"All right." He shrugged and looked away, his eyes shadowed with pain. And Lacey knew she had a choice, refuse to let him see into her past, keep things sterile and professional, or trust him with a little of who she'd been and where she'd come from. Open herself up to hurt. Or maybe to something else. Something she'd only ever dreamed of. Fear held her tongue. Faith loosened it. God hadn't brought her to Lynchburg to see her hurt again. Whatever He planned, whatever He wanted, this was part of it. Lacey knew it as surely as she knew her life was changing. *She* was changing.

She cleared her throat, forcing words past the lump lodged there. "When I was a kid there were plenty of times when I felt just as you do. In pain, wishing I could forget. I worked on my stepfather's farm in Vermont, and the chicken house was the one place I knew no one would look for me. The stench was horrible, but it was safe, so I'd go there when I was hurt, and I'd pretend I was someone else. Not a princess or a superhero, just an ordinary kid with an ordinary life. A kid who had parents who loved her, who lived in a clean house that wasn't filled with anger. A kid who had people in her life who actually cared about her. Of course, pretending never made it so. Eventually, I left Vermont and got a job I loved. A job that allowed me to help other people have ordinary lives. Sick or old or forgotten.

It doesn't matter what their circumstances. I give them as much normalcy as I can. And I let them know they aren't alone."

"The end?" He shifted so he was facing her, his eyes filled with compassion.

"The end."

"I think there's a lot more to the story."

"You're right. There is."

"But you're not going to tell the rest?"

"Not today." She let her hand drop from his waist and stepped away.

"Does that mean never?"

"I don't know." She didn't. She only knew she couldn't tell it now.

"Fair enough. When you're ready, I'll listen, because you're not alone anymore, Lacey, and you don't have to pretend there are people who care. There are." His lips brushed hers, feather light. Barely there, but shaking Lacey to the core.

She jumped back, her fingers pressed against her lips. "Jude—"

"Sorry. Chalk it up to lack of sleep and forget it happened, okay?" He smiled, but there was no mistaking the seriousness in his eyes.

What choice did she have but to agree? "Okay."

"Good. So how about we go inside and have some breakfast?"

"Sure." She followed Jude inside, the pullover she'd brought outside with her clutched in her left hand, her right hand trembling.

Jude had kissed her.

She'd let him.

She wasn't just falling for the man. She'd fallen. And there wasn't a thing she could do about it. She hurried into the laundry room, dropping the pullover onto the pile of clothes there. She needed to pull herself together fast. There was no way she'd fallen for Jude. She refused to even think it, let alone believe it.

"You okay?" Jude peered into the room, his brow furrowed. Obviously, he wasn't nearly as shaken by the kiss as Lacey.

"I'm fine. I was just thinking I'd start a pot of coffee and make a few eggs. Since we didn't get to the grocery store yesterday, you're still short on food. I think I saw some bread in your fridge. I'll get that and…" She took a breath, forced herself to shut her mouth. Blabbering on and on couldn't change what had just happened, and it was only making her look like the nervous wreck she was. "I'll make breakfast. You take some Tylenol. You're not going to make it to your parents' house this afternoon if you can't walk."

"If it weren't for the fact that Grayson and Honor were announcing their engagement today, I think I'd skip out on lunch." He limped to the counter and grabbed the Tylenol, swallowing three dry.

"I'm sure they'd understand. Wait. How did you know what their plans were? Honor said the news was a surprise." She pulled eggs from the fridge, cracked them into a bowl. Anything to keep from looking in Jude's eyes.

"Grayson told me they had news to share. What else could it be?"

"They don't know that you know. If you really aren't well enough—"

"I'll go if I have to use a wheelchair to get there. Grayson is a great guy. He deserves his happiness, and he deserves for me to be there to share it with him." He rubbed the back of his neck and sank into a chair.

"Maybe I should call your doctor. He can call in a prescription for pain medicine."

"Thanks, but I did the pain meds for a month. They fogged my brain and kept me from thinking clearly. That's the last thing I need when I've got someone trying to kill me."

"Has Officer McKnight found any leads?"

"No. What's frustrating is that I keep thinking there was something familiar about the guy who attacked us, but I can't put my finger on what it is."

"We couldn't see his face. Maybe it was his size? His height? His voice?" Lacey offered suggestions as she scrambled the eggs, relaxing now that whatever had passed between her and Jude was over.

"I think it was the way he moved and held his body. He hunched over like an elderly man, but moved like a body-builder. Stiff and tight." Jude shook his head.

"If you're right about recognizing the way the guy moved, then whoever it is must be someone you know well. Someone you see frequently. Not just a person you met at court during a trial."

"That's what's bothering me. I don't want to believe some-one I'm close to would want to kill me, but I keep coming back to the same thing—the person who came after us in the woods was someone I know pretty well. Someone who knows me. Remember when I tried to grab his ski mask?"

"Yes." How could she forget? The entire incident was seared into her mind.

"He kicked my left leg. That's the one the doctors almost couldn't save. Only a few people know how close I came to losing it. Good friends. Coworkers. Family."

"Your list of suspects has changed."

"I know. And I don't like it." He pulled bread from the fridge and slid four pieces into the toaster oven, his expression grim. Lacey almost told him that she understood how he felt, that being betrayed by someone you loved was the worst betrayal of all.

"Did you talk to your friend in New York? Maybe he has some ideas."

"I decided to wait until the sun came up. It's up now. I'll be a few minutes." He grabbed the phone, started walking out of the room.

"Hold on. Your eggs are almost ready."

"I'll eat them when I'm done."

"But—"

Jude was gone before Lacey could finish the sentence. She sighed, spooning fluffy eggs onto a plate, taking the toast out of the oven and spreading it with butter. There wasn't any fruit in the house, but she poured Jude a glass of apple juice, then set everything on the table and waited.

And waited.

And waited.

Finally, she covered the eggs and toast with plastic wrap, put the apple juice in the fridge and cleaned the kitchen. When Jude still hadn't returned, she grabbed her coat and went outside, inhaling the cold air and letting it cool her heated cheeks.

Jude was an adult. He'd eat when he was ready. And she would *not* be sorry that they hadn't sat down to breakfast together. She'd had plenty of clients who preferred to eat their meals alone.

But Jude wasn't just a client. He was becoming something more. Lacey could fight it. She could deny it. But she couldn't change it. She wasn't even sure she wanted to. She frowned, pushing open the door and walking into her duplex. The silence was as comforting as an old friend, and she let it fill her as she jogged up the stairs and started getting ready for church. No matter what happened, God was with her. She wasn't alone. Would never be alone again. That was something she'd carry with her long after her current assignment was over and long after whatever was growing between her and Jude faded.

If it fades.

The thought whispered through her mind, tempting Lacey to believe in forever. She didn't. She wouldn't. But if she dared, she knew what forever would look like. It would look like Jude.

FOURTEEN

Jude watched as Lacey maneuvered Bess into a parking spot at Grace Christian Church and braced himself for what would happen when he got out of the car. Every Sunday for the past three weeks, a half-dozen women had vied for his attention before and after the church service. A few months ago, he would have been flattered by the attention, but things were different now. He was different.

And today he wasn't in the mood to deal with what was becoming more and more a childish game.

After an hour on the phone with Jackson, Jude was more convinced than ever that his hunch was right. The person who'd attacked him in the woods was someone he knew well. The problem was, he was no closer to figuring out who that was. Jackson had promised to ask around, see if anyone on the force had taken a vacation or leave of absence in the past few weeks. He was also going to check in with a few of Jude's rock-climbing buddies. The likelihood that one of his friends was trying to kill him was slim to none, but leaving loose ends and uninvestigated leads had never been Jude's method of investigating.

Frustrated, he shoved open the door, wincing as pain shot up his left thigh. He'd done too much running and walking the previous day, and now he was paying for it. But he'd rather pay than be dead, so Jude guessed he wouldn't complain.

"Do you want more Tylenol?" Lacey pulled a bottle of caplets from her purse and offered them to Jude, the sleeve of her coat riding up to reveal the silvery scars that had been on Jude's mind more and more.

Who had hurt her?

When?

Finding answers to those questions was becoming almost as important to Jude as finding his killer.

Maybe that should have scared him, but it didn't.

Lacey intrigued him, fascinated him. Made him want to know more about who she was and where she'd come from.

"What?" She smoothed her hair, her cheeks pink and silky smooth.

"I was just thinking about how beautiful you look with your hair down."

"Obviously you don't need the Tylenol. You need glasses." She shoved the bottle back in her purse and pushed her door open, but he stopped her before she could get out.

"Wait until I'm out, okay?"

Her eyes widened, and she glanced around the parking lot, understanding immediately what he hadn't said. "You don't think he's here, do you?"

"I don't know, but I don't want you hurt again. If he wants to take a shot at me, let him do so when you're not standing next to me."

"Maybe we should call for a police escort."

"I *am* the police. Remember?" He got out of the car before she could say any more, adrenaline pumping through him at the thought of confronting the person who wanted him dead.

Come on, Lord. Just let him make one careless mistake. That's all I need and I can bring him down and get on with my life. Jude prayed as he got of the car and made a show of getting his Bible out of his trunk.

How long had it been since he'd read it?

Too long.

It was time to change that. Time to start living the life he'd always known he should. If nothing else good came from nearly losing his life, at least he'd have that.

A few people called out and waved as Jude closed the trunk. He waved back, attuned to every movement, every approaching figure. If there was danger nearby, he couldn't feel it.

Finally, he walked around the car, and pulled open the door, offering Lacey a hand out. "We're good."

"You may be, but my heart is about to jump out of my chest." Her palm was smooth and dry, her movements lithe and graceful. She'd worn a dress made of soft, gray fabric that hugged her slender curves and made her skin look silky and smooth. Her lips were pink and unadorned. He'd tasted them earlier, inhaling the delicate fragrance that was Lacey before she'd pulled away. Maybe the kiss had been a mistake, but he didn't regret it. As a matter of fact, he wouldn't have minded kissing her again.

She must have sensed his thoughts.

Her eyes widened, and she took a quick step away, hurrying toward the church building without a second glance in his direction.

He caught up easily, despite the pain in his legs, and hooked an arm around her waist to slow her down. "Are we in a hurry?"

"Being late my first day here won't make a very good impression on the gossips," she answered smoothly, as if there weren't another reason for her quick retreat.

"Gossips, huh?"

"It's as good as an excuse as any for hurrying." She grinned, her eyes flashing with humor, and Jude could imagine doing this with her a million times. Walking into church, his arm around her waist, looking into her eyes while she laughed.

"You should have said you were cold, or that you were worried about being shot in the back. I might have believed either of those."

"No, you wouldn't have. You're too good at reading people to fall for a lie."

"Then why did you try to lie to me?"

"I really don't want to be gossiped about, so what I said wasn't actually a lie."

"It just wasn't the whole truth?"

"Something like that."

"Then what is the truth?"

"You're not like my other clients, Jude."

"What were your other clients like?"

"Predictable."

"You mean boring?"

"No, I mean predictable. I knew what to expect from them and what not to. With you, I've got no idea what's going to happen next."

"What's going to happen next is that we're going to walk into church, and we're going to listen to Pastor Avery's sermon. We'll worry about anything else after I figure out who's trying to kill me." He opened the church door, nudging Lacey inside.

"Just so you know, I'm still not sure there will be something else."

He didn't try to convince her. There'd be time to discuss what was happening between them, but now wasn't it. "Come on. The sanctuary is this way. If I know my brother Grayson he's already there and wondering if he should come back to the house and drag me here."

"Would he really do that?"

"He'd call first. Then he'd drag." That had been how he'd

gotten Jude to church the first week—called him up, told him he'd be at the house in five minutes, and then arrived with Honor and her too-cute kid.

Jude hadn't had any choice but to get dressed and get moving. Grace Christian wasn't the church he'd grown up in, and he had no claim to it, but when he was there, he felt almost as if he belonged. It was a good feeling. One that had convinced him to return week after week.

"Jude! You're here. I saw Grayson come in without you and I was sure something terrible had happened. That you'd had a relapse. I was completely prepared to come over with my famous chicken-noodle soup. It's sure to cure just about any ailment." Millie Andrews glided toward him, her wide brown eyes filled with anticipation.

"No need for that. I'm doing fine." He attempted to sidestep her grasping arms. Newly single after five years of marriage, Millie was desperate for a relationship. Apparently, she'd decided Jude would fit the bill.

A couple of months ago, her sharp good looks would have interested him, and he would have been happy to take her up on her offer. Now he was more interested in a woman of substance and strength. A pretty blond woman of substance and strength.

"Some good chicken soup will still do you good. Why don't I bring it by this afternoon? We can have lunch together." Her smile was filled with sweet charm, but her eyes had a predatory gleam.

"Thanks, but I have plans for this afternoon."

"With who?" She pouted prettily, showing her subtly pink lips to their best advantage.

"Jude and I are having lunch together. I'm Lacey Carmichael." Lacey offered her hand, smiling just as sweetly as Millie had, real amusement in her eyes.

"Oh. I see." Millie frowned, giving Lacey a once-over that couldn't have been more obvious. "I'm Millie Andrews."

"It's nice to meet you, Millie."

"Likewise. Though I had no idea Jude was seeing someone. Have you known each other long?"

"Just two days, but it seems like so much longer. I guess when it's right, it's right." Jude draped an arm over Lacey's shoulders and pulled her into his side, only half pretending. Being with Lacey did seem right, and that was something he'd never felt with another woman.

"I thought the same thing when I married my ex-husband. It didn't take me long to realize that what I'd thought was right was more wrong than I could ever have imagined. See you two lovebirds later." Millie's teeth flashed in what might have been a smile or a grimace before she stalked away.

"Nice. I'm surprised you haven't taken her up on her very obvious offer by now." A hint of laughter colored Lacey's words and sank deep into Jude's heart.

"I guess I was waiting for an offer from someone a little more special."

"Who could be more special than a woman who makes homemade chicken soup and delivers it with a smile?"

"A crocodile smile. Millie is ready to snap her jaws down on any man who gets close."

"That's a perfect description." Lacey laughed and took his hand, pulling him toward the open sanctuary doors. "We'd better get seated before church starts. I wouldn't want your brother to think I'm not doing my job."

"I don't think you have to worry about that. You saved my life. There's nothing you could do that would get you on anyone in my family's bad side."

"I didn't save your life."

"Then what do you call taking a knife that was meant for me?"

"Stupid?"

It was Jude's turn to laugh, and he led her into the sanctuary, feeling better than he had in months. Maybe that came from being with Lacey. Maybe it came from being in church. Jude thought it was a combination of both. Walking into the sanctuary with Lacey made him feel alive and renewed in a way he hadn't in much too long.

"Isn't that Honor and Grayson?" Lacey pointed to a pew near the front of the sanctuary, and Jude nodded, bracing himself for his family's curiosity. They wouldn't ask questions in front of Lacey, but there was no doubt they'd ask eventually.

"Honor's daughter Lily is in children's church. Her sister-in-law Candace attends church at Liberty University. The couple sitting next to Honor is Tristan and Martha. My brother and sister-in-law. My sister and her husband are out of town. You'll meet them next week."

"Your parents aren't here?"

"They live in Forest. It's a half hour from here."

"Maybe I should sit somewhere else, Jude. I hate to intrude on your family."

"Intrude? You're going to be eating lunch with them in a couple of hours."

"I know, but sitting in church with them seems too much like..."

"What?"

"Family."

"That's what they are, Lacey." He stopped a few feet from the pew, trying to read her expression.

"Your family, Jude. Not mine."

"We're in church. Aren't we all the same family?"

"There's a difference, and you know it." She frowned uneasily, her gaze shifting to the pew where Jude's family waited.

"What's different?"

"They're yours, that's what. I'll be a fifth wheel. No one wants to be that."

"Then it's good you could never *be* that." He draped his arm across her shoulders, turning her toward the pew as organ music filled the sanctuary.

His cell phone vibrated as he reached his family, and he accepted hugs from Honor and Martha before glancing at the caller ID.

It was Jackson.

He'd have to take it.

He shook his brothers' hands, urged Lacey to take a seat and then excused himself, limping back up the aisle, knowing that Jack wouldn't have called if he didn't have news.

And knowing deep in his gut that the news wasn't going to make him happy.

FIFTEEN

Lacey had always loved attending church. When she was a kid, she'd loved it because it was the one time during the week when her stepfather wasn't feet away, when she could blend in with a crowd and disappear for a while, lose herself in daydreams and make-believe.

Once she'd left home, she'd enjoyed the serene atmosphere and the camaraderie that came from sharing a common faith. During the years she'd spent traveling from town to town and client to client, the one common denominator had been Sundays spent with people who honored God and trusted in Him. No matter the troubles she was going through, Lacey had never failed to find peace at church on Sunday morning.

Until now.

Squeezed between Grayson Sinclair and the end of the pew, she waited anxiously for Jude's return. Five minutes. Ten. Every second that ticked by felt like an eternity.

Who had the phone call been from?

Why hadn't Jude returned?

Should she go look for him?

She glanced at Grayson, then farther down the pew at Tristan Sinclair. Neither man seemed concerned by his brother's absence. Didn't they understand that Jude was still recovering from his injury? That someone wanted him dead? That at any moment a knife-wielding lunatic could attack him again?

"Keep frowning like that and you'll get wrinkles." Jude nudged her over, dropping into the pew beside her.

"Is everything okay?" She leaned close to whisper in his ear, inhaling cold air and Jude. Something deep in her soul shivered in response.

"No, but we'll discuss it after church." He shifted so that his arm was lying against the back of the pew, his hand resting on her shoulder. Casually connecting them.

Ignore it.

Ignore him.

But she couldn't ignore Jude any more than she could ignore a hurricane-force wind.

The pastor began to speak, but Lacey's mind wasn't on the message. It was on escape. She wanted to jump up and run from the church. Run from Lynchburg. Run from Jude and all the feelings he'd sparked to life inside her.

"Relax," Jude whispered in her ear. His hand stroked down her shoulder then back up to rest lightly against her neck. Warm flesh against chilled. Quiet confidence against anxiety. Obviously, Jude had no problem believing in dreams and happiness. And sitting there next to him, his arm heavy against her back, his hand light against her neck, she wanted to believe, too.

Stupid. That's what you are, Lacey Beth. Asking for trouble. Begging for trouble. And that's exactly what you're going to get.

The voice from the past hissed its poison, the memory of it like ice water in Lacey's veins. She shivered, shifting away from Jude and bumping into Grayson. He glanced her way, lifting an eyebrow.

"Sorry."

But he'd already turned his attention back to the sermon, his hand linked with Honor's, his thumb caressing her knuckles. A couple enjoying church together and preparing to make a lifetime commitment to one another. That was the way it was supposed to be, right? A man and woman found each other, fell in love and spent their lives building dreams together.

As easy as one, two, three.

But not so easy for Lacey.

She shivered again.

"Cold?" Jude moved closer, oblivious to Lacey's discomfort.

She shook her head, but didn't speak.

What could she say?

That the past still haunted her? That no matter how much she might want to believe she'd put it behind her, she had never quite let go of the pain she'd suffered?

When she'd been a kid, one of Lacey's chores had been to whitewash the fence that surrounded her stepfather's property. Over the years, the old wood fence became warped and rotted, but Uriah refused to replace any of the boards. Instead, he sent Lacey out with gallons of white paint and a brush and set her to work in the hot summer sun. One stroke of paint after another hid the warped and rotted wood, but nothing could change what it was.

Sometimes Lacey felt like that old fence. Shiny and new on the outside, but littered with holes and rot underneath.

"We are called to live for God. In this moment. Not in the past or in the future. Whatever you are clinging to today, let it go and step forward into what God has planned for you *now*."

The pastor's words seeped into Lacey's thoughts, hit deep in her soul where the ugliness of the past dug its sharp talons.

Let it go.

If only it were that easy.

If only she could wish it away, pray it away, believe it away.

Maybe then she could find what Honor and Grayson had. Maybe then she'd finally have a place to go home to.

The final notes of the last hymn faded away, and Jude took her hand. "Ready to go?"

"Sure."

"Gray?" He leaned past Lacey, pulling her closer as he spoke to his brother, his heat seeping through Lacey's sweater dress, warming the chill that had taken up residence in her soul.

"Yeah?" Grayson replied.

"I've got to go to the Lynchburg PD station. I have some information McKnight is going to want. Tell Mom and Dad I'll be a little late, but I'll be there."

"You going to tell us what this is about?" Tristan Sinclair scowled at Jude, and Lacey had the feeling he wasn't the kind of man anyone would want to tangle with.

"I'm sure McKnight has already filled Grayson in. I'll let him tell you."

"That someone is trying to kill you and you didn't bother mentioning it to us?" Tristan growled the words, and Jude stiffened.

"News travels fast in this family."

"It would have traveled faster if you'd had the decency to tell us what you suspected, bro." Grayson's tone was more controlled than his siblings', but there was no mistaking his anger.

"I didn't want to drag you into my mess."

"Drag us? We would have jumped in feet first and looked to see if there was something under us later. I can't believe—"

"Tristan?" His pretty, blond-haired wife put a hand on his arm. "Why don't we talk about this at your parents' place after everyone has had time to think about what he wants to say?"

"If by 'everyone' you mean me, that's probably a good idea." Tristan dropped a kiss on his wife's forehead, and turned back to Jude. "We'll talk later. In the meantime, be careful."

"That goes without saying."

"Apparently, a lot of things go without saying with you." Having made his parting shot, Tristan waved goodbye to Lacey and stalked away. Grayson and Honor followed seconds later.

"Sorry about that." Jude's scowl was so like his brother Tristan's, Lacey smiled.

"Sorry about what?"

"My brothers can be overbearing."

"But they mean well."

"Yeah, they do."

"There are a lot of people who would give everything to have people who care about them the way your brothers care about you."

"Are you one of them?" He pressed his hand to her lower back, urging her out into the aisle where a hundred or so people were moving toward the door.

"I don't think there is anyone alive who doesn't want someone to care about her."

"You're good at avoiding my questions."

"And you're good at asking them."

"I'm interested in you, and I'm not going to hide the way I feel."

"The way you feel? We've only known each other a couple of days. How can you feel anything?"

But she knew, because she felt it, too. The tug of awareness, the electricity in the air when they were close to each other.

"Look." Jude stopped short, his eyes blazing. "I understand that you're scared. I understand that you're not ready for a relationship. But I won't let you lie to yourself or to me. You feel the same thing I do. Whether or not something comes of it, whether or not you want something to come of it is a different story, but at least admit you feel it."

She couldn't lie. Wouldn't lie. "You're right. I do."

"I knew you had it in you." He grinned and started walking again.

"What?"

"Courage."

"Courage? An hour ago, you said I saved your life. A coward wouldn't have done that."

"I didn't say you were a coward. You're plenty brave enough when it comes to fighting for other people. It's fighting for yourself you have a problem with."

"I—" But he was right, and Lacey fell silent as they stepped outside into the cold gray afternoon.

"There's no need to look so grim," Jude said, as he opened the car door. "I'm not going to kidnap you and hold you hostage until you agree we're meant to be together."

Lacey froze, half in the car, half out, her heart beating so hard and fast, she was sure it would burst. Did he know about her past? "Why would you say that?"

He'd been smiling, but it fell away, his gaze sharpening, his jaw suddenly tense. "It was a joke, but I can see you don't think it's funny."

"You're right. I don't. Too many stories in the news about people doing stuff like that." She tried to lighten her tone and her expression, but the damage was already done.

"When did it happen, Lacey? Who was it?" Jude's eyes flashed with anger, and Lacey knew that she couldn't avoid the questions. This time Jude would keep asking. If she wasn't willing to answer, he'd find someone who was.

"A long time ago. So long ago, I barely even think about it any more."

"Liar." He growled the word, but there was pity in his eyes. Pity Lacey didn't want or need.

"My stepfather was a sociopath. He liked to control everyone and everything in his life. I was a rebel who refused to be controlled." She shrugged. "It got ugly, but I survived. Now, if we're done discussing my past, we've got to get moving. You said you needed to go to the Lynchburg police department, and your parents aren't going to want to hold lunch forever."

"What happened to your stepfather? Is he still alive, because if he is—"

"You can stop the macho protective thing. When I needed help, there wasn't any. It's too late to change that now." She'd spent four days in a sweltering barn, handcuffed and chained to a wooden post, yanking and pulling at her bonds until her wrists bled, the fetid sores weeping tears Lacey had refused to shed.

"Is. He. Still. Alive?"

Jude's anger took her by surprise and knocked the breath from her lungs. She remembered a lot of things from the day she'd finally broken free. She remembered yanking one last time at the chains, praying God would help her and knowing that if He didn't she would die. She remembered the wooden post giving way, falling toward her and pinning her beneath its weight. Then her mother coming from the house, screaming that Uriah would have Lacey's head for destroying his barn. Everything else was a blur. The paramedics and police coming because Lacey's mother couldn't pull her free from the rubble. The police staring at her with shock and pity. The feeling of hot sunshine and fresh air. Of freedom.

What she didn't remember was anyone being angry for her.

"Is he alive?" Jude spoke more gently this time, his hand shaking as he brushed hair from Lacey's cheek and lay his palm against her skin.

And for the first time in too many years to count, tears burned at the back of Lacey's eyes.

Babies cry, Lacey Beth. And you're no baby. You either take your punishment with silence, or I'll give you more of the same.

She blinked the tears away, her stomach churning, a hollow ache in her heart reminding her of what she'd wanted so desperately when she was young. Someone to depend on. "Uriah is in jail. He'll be there for the rest of his life."

"What—"

"You can ask me more questions, but I won't answer them, so how about we just go?"

His jaw tightened, but he nodded, his movements stiff as he closed the door and walked around the car.

She thought he would say something when he got in and braced herself for it.

Instead, his silence filled the car as she headed for Lynchburg, the sound of it louder than any words could have been. Tight-jawed and tense, he stared at the road, his pulse beating rapidly in his throat.

What was he thinking?

Did Lacey really want to know?

No.

Yes.

But she wouldn't ask because asking would open up another conversation about her past.

She'd said enough about that already.

She shifted uncomfortably, wanting to say something but sure anything she said would just lead back to a place she didn't want to go.

SIXTEEN

Jude wanted to break something.

Correction.

He wanted to break *someone*.

Uriah. Lacey's stepfather.

Was his last name Carmichael or something else?

Jude planned to find out, and then he planned to pay a visit to whatever jail cell the scumbag was living in.

"What are you planning to talk to Officer McKnight about?" Lacey sounded tentative and unsure, and that made Jude even more angry than he already was.

Kidnapped. Held hostage.

His hands tightened into fists, and he imagined wrapping them around Uriah's neck.

"Jude? I..." Lacey touched his wrist, her fingers barely there before they fell away again.

"What?" He waited until she pulled into the parking lot of the Lynchburg police department and turned to face her. Her face was pale, her eyes deep-green and filled with anxiety she couldn't hide.

"Nothing has changed. I'm still me. My past was my past before you knew about it."

"You're wrong, Lacey. Everything has changed. That line

you were so worried about crossing? I crossed it the day I met you. Everything I learn about you just pulls me that much further over it."

"I don't want to talk about this right now."

"Then when?"

"Never." She pushed open her door, but Jude grabbed her hand, stopping her before she could get out of the car.

"You can't run from your past forever."

"Sure I can." She flashed a brittle smile and yanked away.

He let her go.

Pressuring her to let him into her life would be a mistake. If there was going to be anything between them, it had to be on Lacey's terms. Jude knew it. He just didn't like it.

She tensed as he fell into step beside her. Probably expecting him to bring up their relationship or the past again. A few months ago, he would have. Nearly dying had changed him. It had forced patience on to him and into him, and he had a feeling that was going to serve him well when it came to Lacey.

God's plan?

Jude was beginning to think so. He'd walked away from God years ago, but God had never turned away from him.

The thought stilled some of the wild anger in his gut. He took a deep breath, allowing himself to feel the cold winter wind and to inhale the scent of spring rain and flowers that swirled around Lacey. "My friend in New York called me with a lead."

At his words, Lacey relaxed, the anxiety in her eyes fading. "That's good news."

"Good for me if it turns out to lead somewhere. Not so good for the guy it's leading to."

"Who is it leading to?"

"An old sergeant of mine. I worked for him before I moved to Homicide. Five years ago."

"That's a long time."

"It is. He wasn't even on my radar. Fortunately, Jackson decided to dig a little deeper than I would have. He found out Jimmy took a leave of absence four months ago."

"Does Jackson know why?"

"There was a death in the family. Jimmy's seventeen-year-old son died at a boot camp in Arizona."

"That's terrible."

"It is. The kid had been in and out of trouble for years. As a matter of fact, I brought him into the station three times the year I worked for Jimmy. The kid shoplifted, went for a joyride and grabbed an elderly woman's bag. He was only twelve at the time."

"Sounds like he was really troubled."

"That's what I told Jim. I recommended the treatment program out in Arizona, thinking it might help straighten the kid out."

"You don't think Jim held that against you?"

"I don't know. Once I find him, I'll ask."

"Maybe you'll find him today. Maybe today will be the day you get the answers you've been looking for these past two months."

"It would make my life a whole lot less dangerous if that were the case." He held open the precinct door, and Lacey stepped through ahead of him.

"Will you go back to New York after this is over? Finish your rehab there?"

"That was my plan, but the thought of going back to the city doesn't appeal to me as much as I thought it would. I want to go back into police work, but there are other places to do it."

"Places closer to family?"

"Yes." He flashed his badge at the desk sergeant and asked to speak to Officer McKnight before he turned his attention back to Lacey. "Nearly dying taught me a lot about what's important. The freedom and independence I gained by moving to

New York weren't worth the distance it put between myself and my family."

"Detective Sinclair?" Officer McKnight stepped into the lobby. "Come on back. You can come along, too, Ms. Carmichael. A few things have come up in the investigation, and I want to ask you some questions about them."

A few things?

Ask some questions?

Lacey tensed, her stomach tying into knots as she followed Jude and Officer McKnight to a small cubicle. She'd thought she was done answering questions when Jude changed the subject.

Apparently she'd been wrong.

What kind of questions could the officer possibly want her to answer?

She knew, though.

Her past.

No matter how hard she tried to do what the pastor had said and put it behind her, it kept rearing its ugly head and making itself known.

"Have a seat." He motioned to two chairs, then took a seat across from them. "What is it you wanted to discuss, Sinclair?"

"I've gotten some information you might be interested in. I thought I'd share."

"Go ahead."

Jude spoke quickly, sharing the same story and details he'd shared with Lacey. She only half listened, her heart still racing way too fast, her stomach tied in knots.

Why, Lord? After all these years, why does this all have to be coming up now?

Because she had never truly put the past behind her.

Lacey knew the answer without hearing God speak it.

Then again, she *had* heard Him. When she'd listened to Pastor Avery, the message had gone straight to her heart.

"That's a promising lead, Sinclair, but I'm not sure I want it to pan out." Officer McKnight's rough voice pulled Lacey from her thoughts and back to the conversation.

"I feel the same."

"I'll send some men to visit local hotels after I have your precinct send me a file photo of your sergeant. Until then, be careful." He turned his dark gaze on Lacey, and she knew what was coming.

"Ms. Carmichael—"

"Lacey." After all, he knew more about her life than most people.

"Lacey, I was doing some research yesterday, just kind of putting some feelers out. Found the name Uriah Carmichael in the national database."

"My stepfather."

"He's been in jail for twelve years."

"That's right."

"Do you have any reason to believe he would send somebody after you? Any reason to suspect what happened yesterday has something to do with your past?"

"No."

"I called the Vermont state police. Talked to a couple of guys who worked…the case twelve years ago." He glanced at Jude, maybe worried about protecting Lacey's privacy.

Too late.

"I'm sure they told you that I haven't had any contact with anyone in my family for years."

"They also said your stepbrother made overt threats before and after his father's trial."

"I thought you said you didn't have any siblings." Jude's voice was tight with anger, and Lacey wasn't sure if it was directed at her or at what had happened years ago.

"I don't. My stepbrother was a grown man by the time my

mother married my stepfather. We didn't have all that much to do with each other."

Jude's dark gaze shot to Officer McKnight. "What kind of threats did he make against her, McKnight? Why do you think they might be connected to what's happening now?"

McKnight hesitated, his eyes troubled as he looked at Lacey. He knew. Knew everything. Every shameful, horrifying detail of the nightmare she'd lived. "I don't, but I have to check it out. I'm sure you understand that, Lacey."

"I do."

"We've got the local police looking for your stepbrother. If we find him in Vermont, we can assume yesterday's attack has nothing to do with him."

"It doesn't. Shane was more interested in putting on a show than in taking action. That was his MO in life. I'm sure it still is. If he ran into me tomorrow, he might make threats, but he'd never act on them."

"How about you let us decide whether or not that's the case?" McKnight's scribbled notes on a pad of paper, typed something into his computer and stood. "That's it, then. You've got as much information as I do. I'll keep you posted on the investigation."

"You do that." Jude's words were tight, his face hard. Lacey was sure he would have a lot more to say about her stepbrother.

Unfortunately for him, she didn't.

She smiled at Officer McKnight, doing her best to look relaxed and at ease. As if the past hadn't punched holes into her heart and left it with ragged bleeding wounds that would never heal. "Thank you for all your help, Officer."

"Thank me by being careful. We've been working under the assumption that Jude was the target of yesterday's attack. Now I'm not so sure."

"You can be. There is no way Shane Carmichael would

waste energy coming after me. As far as he was concerned, I was as insignificant as a flea on a dog's behind."

Jude's eyes widened at her words, his lips twitched and then he laughed. Loud and warm and without apology. "Watch it, Lacey. Your country is coming out."

"What's wrong with country?"

"On you? Nothing." He grabbed her hand, his touch warm and strong, pulling her from the past and into something she didn't dare believe in.

She went anyway.

Willingly.

Like a lamb to the slaughter.

Lamb to a slaughter?

Not good.

Lacey tugged her hand away, putting some distance between them. "I've been thinking."

"Do I want to know what about?"

She ignored his gentle teasing. "Your legs seem to be feeling better than they were this morning."

"They are."

"So I thought maybe I could have the afternoon off."

He didn't respond, and Lacey hurried to fill in the silence. "It's in my contract, Jude. I get Sunday afternoons off."

"I remember."

"So why aren't you saying anything?"

"Because I haven't thought of a reasonable excuse for refusing your request."

"Why would you want to?"

"Why do you think, Lacey?"

"I don't know."

But she did, and the truth of it burned through her defenses, demanding her attention.

"Sure you do. You've already admitted you feel something

for me. Why should you be surprised that I want to spend more time with you?"

Her breath caught, and she shook her head. "Whatever I feel? It's just that. A feeling. I'll get over it. So will you."

"Why should we? What's wrong with spending time together and seeing where it leads?"

Nothing.

Everything.

Except that Lacey wanted it so badly.

"I want the afternoon off, Jude. That's all. No hidden agenda. No deep, dark reasons for it. I need a break. Is that so hard to understand?" She fled down the hall, past the desk sergeant and out the door, the lie ringing in her ears, mocking her.

She didn't need a break.

She needed Jude.

And that was scarier than her stepfather, her stepbrother and a masked killer all put together.

SEVENTEEN

Jude followed Lacey outside, breathing in the cold, moist air, filling his lungs with it and doing his best to calm the wild beating of his heart. Hearing Lacey's story, knowing how deeply she'd been hurt, only made him admire her more. It also made him realize how careful he needed to be with her. What he wanted out of their relationship paled in comparison to what Lacey needed—friendship, tenderness, security. Jude would give her all those things. If she'd let him.

She stood beside his car, her back to him as he approached, but he knew she heard him. Her shoulders tensed, and she wrapped her arms around her waist.

"If you're going to try and convince me that I shouldn't take the afternoon off, then don't waste your breath."

"I'm not."

"Good, because I'm really tired and I really do need a break." She turned to him, her face colorless, her eyes hollow and empty. For the first time since he'd met her, she looked like what she'd been—a victim.

He smoothed silky strands of hair from her face, his hands shaking with anger over what had been done to her. His heart breaking for her. He'd spent most of his adult life working to defend the defenseless, to find justice for victims who could not fight for themselves. He wanted to do that for Lacey. Defend her. Protect her.

But how do you defend against an invisible enemy? How do you protect against the past?

He sighed, pulling her into his arms, pressing her head to his chest, her hair sliding over his hand and down his arm. "I'm not going to ask you any more questions. Your secrets are yours to keep for as long as you want to."

"My past isn't a secret anymore, so I guess you can ask me any questions you want." She shrugged, her arms wrapping around his waist, holding him for just a second before she stepped away.

"I'm not talking about your past. I'm talking about us."

"Us? I wish I believed in that as much as you do." She frowned, turning away again. "When I was little, I used to dream I'd marry a handsome prince."

"Did you?" He cupped her shoulder, feeling tight muscles and delicate bones beneath her wool coat.

"I thought he'd be brave and strong and kind. And rich, of course."

Jude couldn't see her face, but he was sure Lacey was smiling at the memory. He wasn't, because in his mind he pictured a neglected kid with flaxen hair and big green eyes, sitting alone in a crumbling house and dreaming of something better.

His stomach knotted.

"Of course, I grew out of that. Eventually, I realized that life was about hard work and survival. It was about seeking God's will and about doing it. It wasn't about love and romance and a handsome man who would love me forever."

"I understand."

"Do you?" She shifted beneath his hands, turning so that they were face-to-face. "Because I don't dream anymore, Jude. It hurts too much."

"Lacey—"

"My hand is really bothering me. I'd like to go back to the duplex and take something for it."

Jude didn't mention the Tylenol he knew Lacey was carrying in her purse. She needed space. The best thing he could do was give it. "Sure. Hop in."

He pulled the door open, waited until she got in and closed it, freezing when he heard a quiet shuffle coming from somewhere behind him.

He turned slowly, his hand on the gun hidden beneath his jacket.

Nothing.

Nobody.

But the afternoon was as still and silent as death. Jude's nerves crawled and adrenaline pumped through him. A warning he wouldn't ignore.

"Come on. Show yourself. Right here in front of the police station. Or are you too much of a coward for that?" He muttered the words and didn't expect a reply.

"Jude?" Lacey opened her door and started getting out of the car. "Is everything okay?"

"Get back in the car."

Her eyes widened, but she did as he said, closing the door, the quiet *click* breaking whatever spell had fallen over the day. Rain began to fall, splashing onto the pavement, filling the silence. A uniformed officer walked out of the building, and Jude knew whoever had been in the parking lot was gone.

He frowned, glancing around and spotting two security cameras. They might have picked something up. He dialed McKnight's cell phone, giving him the details of what had happened as Lacey pulled out of the parking lot.

"Do you really think someone was there?" Lacey asked, as he shoved his cell phone back in his pocket.

"Yeah."

"Then the guy is crazy. What kind of criminal goes to a police station to commit a crime?"

"It isn't a crime to watch someone, and I don't think he's crazy. I think he's getting desperate. He wants me dead and he wants it to happen soon."

"Maybe he thinks you're getting close to finding him."

"If that's the case, he should act again soon."

"I don't think I like that idea."

"You won't have to worry about it. I want you on a plane and out of town tomorrow."

"Sounds like a great plan, but where would I go?"

"Home."

"Whatever job I'm at is home, Jude. *This* is my home. For the next month. Then I'll start a new job and start all over again."

"So, we'll find somewhere for you to go until your contract with Grayson is up. You can't stay around me. It's too dangerous."

"Like where? With a friend of yours? Your family? I wouldn't be comfortable doing that." Lacey pulled up in front of the duplex and turned to face him.

"Then where *would* you be comfortable?"

She glanced outside the window, a half smile curving her lips. "I don't know, but of all the places I've been in the past ten years, this is the closest I've found to home."

There were a lot of things Jude could have said about that. He kept them all to himself. He didn't want to scare Lacey away; he just wanted to keep her safe. "I'll ask around. There's probably a rental somewhere close by that you can stay in until this is all sorted out."

"I can't take your brother's money and not work, Jude. I'll have to call Helping Hands tomorrow and tell them what's going on. I'm sure they'll refund Grayson's money and find me another job." She got out of the car and Jude followed.

"Where?"

"Wherever they decide I'd be a good fit." She smiled as she unlocked her door. "Don't look so gloomy. You're getting what you want."

"Not even close."

"You fired me hours after we met, remember? You should be happy to get me out from under your feet."

"There's only one thing that could make me happy right now, Lacey."

"Finding the guy who's trying to kill you?"

"No. This." He didn't think, just acted, pressing his lips to Lacey's, kissing her with passion and with need.

She gasped, then sank into the embrace, her hands wrapping around his waist and pulling him close.

Breathless, he broke away, looking down into Lacey's eyes and seeing what he'd known he had all along—forever.

"That wasn't a good idea, Jude." Her fingers trembled against her lips, and she stepped back, bumping against the front door.

"Funny, I was thinking it was a great idea." He stepped back, knowing that if he didn't he would reach for her again. "Here, take my house key. I've got some stuff in my cupboards if you're hungry."

"Hungry?"

"You haven't eaten since breakfast, and we haven't gone to the store for groceries, so I'm pretty sure your cupboards are still empty."

"They are, but—"

"I've got soup. Probably some crackers, too. It's not as good as Mom's cooking, but at least you won't go hungry."

"Thanks, Jude, but I have a car. I can get whatever I need."

"You shouldn't be driving around while your hand is in bandages." He pressed the key into her palm, and she pushed it back to him.

"I can't take this. You'll need it to get back into your house."

"Then I guess you'd better still be around when I come home." He grinned, and Lacey laughed, shaking her head.

"Ah, your evil plot is revealed. You're giving me your key to keep me from running away."

"I wouldn't say it was evil."

"Devious, then."

"Much better word choice." He nudged Lacey toward the door. "Go on inside. If I'm not there soon, my family will send out a posse."

"It must be nice to be loved like that."

"It is."

"You're really blessed, Jude. I hope you realize that." She smiled and stepped inside her house, closing the door and leaving Jude standing alone on the porch, her words echoing in his ears.

You're really blessed.

Coming from anyone else, the comment could have been taken as sarcasm. After everything Jude had been through, there were a lot of people who'd think he was cursed. But Lacey was right: The good in his life far outweighed the bad.

He limped down the porch steps and got in his car, glancing up at the house as he backed down the driveway. Lacey was standing in the living room window, silently watching his retreat, her hand pressed against her lips as if she could still feel their kiss.

Jude sure could.

He waved and she responded, lifting her white bandaged hand. A victim again.

Jude frowned as he pulled around a curve in the driveway and lost sight of the house. Lacey had been hurt too many times in her life. He'd do everything in his power to make sure she wasn't hurt again. Even if that meant saying goodbye to her.

For a little while, at least. Just until it was safe for her to come back and start building that forever that he wanted with her.

He lifted his cell phone and dialed his parents' number. It would be good to check in and let them know he was running later than expected. And while he was at it, he would put a bug in his mother's ear, tell her that Lacey was going to need a place to stay until her company came through with a new assignment.

Where would they send her?

Back to Chicago? Or somewhere even farther?

The thought didn't make Jude happy, but being happy wasn't what it was about. Keeping Lacey safe was.

"Hello?" His mother's voice filled the line.

"It's me. I'm running late."

"Grayson told us you would be."

"I'll be there in half an hour."

"I'll try to keep your brothers and father from eating all the food before you and Lacey get here."

"Lacey won't be coming."

"Did you scare her away already, Jude?"

"I didn't even try."

"I was hoping you'd say that." Jude could picture his mother's smile and knew she was imagining another wedding and a few more grandkids.

"There is a problem, though."

"What's that?"

He explained, leaving out as much as he could about the danger he was in. When he finished, his mother was silent.

"You still there, Mom?"

"Just thinking."

"About?"

"How much I don't want you to get hurt again. Sitting at your side while you were in the hospital was one of the hardest things I've ever done."

"I'll be okay."

"I pray you're right. I just hope that's enough."

"It'll be plenty. God has looked out for me this far. I don't think He's going to turn away now."

"You're right." She sighed. "I was thinking something else, too."

"What's that?"

"How wonderful a December wedding would be. Your father and I were married in December."

"Don't put the cart before the horse, Mom. Lacey and I aren't even dating."

"Not yet."

"Mom—"

"All right, I'll drop the subject, and I'll start making calls. I'm sure we'll be able to find a place for Lacey to stay."

"Thanks, Mom."

"And, Jude?"

"Yes."

"Please, be careful."

"I will." He tossed the phone onto the passenger's seat, squinting as the sun shot out from behind thick clouds. Bright and warm. A promise of the coming spring.

He planned to be around when the seasons changed. When the weather warmed and the lake turned blue-green, he'd ship his canoe from New York and explore the hushed coves and quiet sanctuaries of the lake.

He could picture it now—water lapping against the boat, the rising sun shimmering on the surface of the lake. Lacey across from him, her blond hair braided and falling over her shoulder, her cheeks pink from warmth and pleasure.

A great dream.

Jude just prayed he could stay alive long enough to make it come true.

EIGHTEEN

Lacey lifted a tulip bulb and pressed it into loose, moist earth, her right arm aching from hours of one-handed hoeing. She didn't mind. A little pain was worth it for what she'd accomplished, and she wasn't talking about the tiny garden plot she'd managed to hack out of the overgrown earth in her backyard. Keeping busy had kept her from dwelling on the things that had chased her from room to room after Jude left.

The past.

Jude.

His kiss.

The one that had stolen her breath and her heart.

She frowned, stabbing a spade into the earth, scooping out dirt and placing a bulb inside. The kiss had *not* stolen her heart. And neither had Jude.

"And he won't."

Liar. He already has.

The truth whispered through her mind, but she ignored it, scooping up more earth, planting another bulb.

Come spring, the garden would bloom with color, but Lacey wouldn't be there to see it. Over the years, she'd planted a garden at almost every house she'd worked in, and it had never bothered her to leave the gardens behind. Things were different this time. She wanted to be around when these tulips bloomed and the little apple tree she'd bought blossomed. She wanted to inhale spring while she nursed a cup of coffee on the brick patio outside the sliding glass door.

She wanted to take that canoe ride with Jude and come back home to talk about what they'd seen.

She wanted so much more than she should.

She sighed, brushing a stray wisp of hair from her cheek and surveyed her work. The little plot looked good. Maybe the next tenant would nurture it and help it grow.

The next tenant.

If Lacey could have, she would have been that person.

Home wasn't something she'd ever believed in, but when she looked into Jude's eyes, she saw it. Tempting her to hope for things she knew she shouldn't want. A place where she belonged. Someone to come home to. Arms that offered comfort and support.

Jude.

She was back to him again.

"That's not good, Lord. We both know it. You've given me a good life, a good job. I've got real opportunities to help people who don't have anyone else. I can't afford to get caught up in a relationship."

Sure you can. You're just afraid to let it happen.

The words whispered on the wind, swirling around Lacey and inside her.

She *was* afraid.

She'd learned what relationships cost—everything.

That was too much to pay.

A raindrop splashed against her cheek and slid down her jaw like an icy finger, pulling her attention back to the little yard and tiny garden. Rain again. She hadn't even noticed the darkening sky. Heavy clouds pressed close to the earth, casting the world in an eerie gray light. Lacey shivered, grabbing the spade and turning back to the house.

A soft shuffling sound carried over the patter of rain, and she froze, a warning tripping along her spine, doing a tap dance in her brain.

Danger.

She backed toward the sliding glass door one slow step at a time, her gaze on the back gate. The six-foot privacy fence hid whatever was on the other side, but Lacey had no trouble imagining it. A man, of course. Tall, slightly hunched. Ski mask over his face.

She wanted to turn and run but was afraid to have her back to danger.

The sliding glass door slid open beneath her questing fingers, and she stepped inside, pulling the door shut and locking it as the gate at the rear of her backyard slowly swung open. She screamed, jumping backward and grabbing for the phone, her hands shaking, the phone slipping from her fingers and clattering onto the ground.

She lifted it, her gaze on the gate. A dark figure walked through it. Tall. Slim and muscular. Five o'clock shadow. Piercing gray eyes.

Jude.

She dropped the phone on the counter and pulled open the door, not sure whether she wanted to strangle or hug him. "What were you thinking, coming through the back gate? You scared me nearly to death."

"I knocked on your door, but you didn't answer. I figured I'd come around the back and knock on the sliding glass door." He stepped into the house, brushing drops of rain from his face and hair. "Looks like you were doing some yard work."

"Just a little."

"And I didn't even want you driving with that bandaged

hand. Let me see." He lifted her hand, frowning at the dirt that speckled the bandage. "This is going to have to be changed."

"I'll do it later."

"How about we do it now? Do you have gauze?"

"In one of those bags." She gestured to the plastic bags she still hadn't unpacked. "But I'll take care of it."

He ignored her and opened the first bag, pulling out a package of mini candy bars and a bottle of diet Coke. "Diet soda and candy?"

"Why not?"

"Why?" He looked in the next bag, smirking as he pulled out a box of Twinkies. "For me?"

She wanted to say no, but that would have been a lie. "You asked me to buy some."

"I also asked you to check out the big screen TVs. Do you have one of those in here, too?"

"I don't like you that much."

He laughed, setting the Twinkies on the counter and pulling out gauze and alcohol. "Ready?"

"Not really."

"You're not scared, are you?" He washed his hands, then sat down beside her, carefully unwrapping her hand.

"Of getting a bandage changed? No."

Of having Jude so close? Yes!

It didn't take long for Jude to clean the wound and change the bandage, and that was a good thing, because Lacey's brain didn't seem to function when he was so close. As soon as he finished, she jumped up and grabbed a paper cup from the cupboard. "Root beer?"

"No. Thanks."

"Suit yourself." She poured herself diet Coke and grabbed a couple of mini candy bars.

"If you eat that, it'll ruin your dinner."

"This *is* my dinner."

"I guess that means you don't want the leftovers my mom sent for you."

"Leftovers?" She set the candy bars down. It had been a long time since she'd eaten a meal cooked by someone else. Unless she counted chefs at restaurants, which she didn't.

"Pot roast. Homemade dinner rolls. Apple pie. I've got ice cream in my fridge to go with it."

Just hearing the food described was enough to make Lacey's mouth water. "So maybe I don't need the candy after all."

"The food is out in my car. I'll get it in a minute." He stretched his legs out and winced.

"It's okay. Stay put. I'll do it."

"Let's do it together after I rest my legs, okay? I don't want you out front alone."

"You've overdone it the past few days. Why don't you go over to your place and sit in the recliner? We can ice your legs and see if that helps."

"*We* aren't going to ice anything." He scowled, his eyes flashing with irritation.

"It was just a suggestion."

"Maybe you can make another one?"

"You could tell me how things went at your parents'. Did you act appropriately surprised when Grayson and Honor announced their engagement?"

"I was pretty convincing if I do say so myself."

"I'll have to ask your mother later and see what she says."

"She's going to say exactly what I did, that I was more surprised than anyone. Including my father, who couldn't quite wrap his mind around the fact that he's got to put on a suit again."

"He doesn't like wearing suits?"

"He's more a polo-and-khakis type of guy." He shifted in the chair and winced.

"Jude, I really do think we need to ice your legs. If the muscles are knotted, I can—"

"There is no way you're going to give me a leg massage."

"Why not?"

"Because you're a woman and I'm a man."

"So? Haven't you ever had a female doctor or nurse or physical therapist?"

"That's different."

"Why?"

"Because none of them were you."

Exasperated, Lacey got up and grabbed one of the candy bars. "You know something, Jude? You're as stubborn as the old mule Mother kept penned out behind our house. She bought him thinking she'd bring him to birthday parties and let kids ride him, but Old Joe wouldn't have anything to do with it, no matter how many carrots she dangled in front of his nose."

"So what happened to poor Old Joe?"

"Mom beat him with a stick after every birthday party, and I snuck him carrots to make him feel better."

"Sounds like you had a soft spot for that stubborn donkey."

"I did." She pulled a chair over and eased Jude's feet onto it. "But that doesn't mean I have one for you."

"Sure you do. You just don't know it yet." He grinned, and Lacey knew she was smiling like an empty-headed twit.

What was it about Jude that made her forget the rule? The one that clearly stated Lacey would not have men in her life. Ever.

"At least take some Tylenol, Jude." She grabbed a bottle from her cupboard and poured three into his hand.

He swallowed them and let his feet drop off the chair. "There. Happy?"

"I'd be happier if you'd let me help you more."

"You've helped me plenty. Come on. Let's go get those leftovers."

"There's no rush."

"Sure there is. My mother will be calling you any minute to see if the food has been delivered. If it hasn't, she'll cut me off of home-cooked meals for good."

"No way."

"It's what she said. And my mother doesn't make idle threats." He limped out of the room, his discomfort so obvious, Lacey rushed forward and put an arm around his waist.

"I think we should call your doctor first thing in the morning and get an appointment for you to be seen."

"Sorry. I've got plans."

"What kind of plans?"

"Finding-a-killer plans." He limped down the stairs, and Lacey went with him.

"You're not going to be in any shape to find the guy if you don't take it easy."

"I'll manage." He pulled two bags out of the back of his car and handed one to Lacey. "That's yours. It's got the extra pie."

"You're not going to distract me by mentioning pie, you know."

"So how about I distract you by telling you how pretty you look in yellow?" He eyed her appreciatively, his silvery gaze touching on the sunny yellow turtleneck and jeans she'd changed into after church. Both were faded and soft with age, but the way Jude looked at them, they could have been the finest silk.

"Flattery will get you nowhere, Jude. And it certainly won't convince me to change the subject."

"I kind of thought that. Unfortunately, the subject is going to have to stay closed. I want to call Jack, see if he's found out anything else about Jim."

"And you're going to put your feet up while you do it?"

"For you? Sure." He smiled, hooking his arm around her waist and walking back to the house. "I think you still have my key."

"Right here." She fished it from her pocket and placed it in Jude's palm.

He wrapped his fingers around her hand before she could pull away, his thumb brushing over the tender flesh on the underside of her wrist. "My phone call can wait for a little while if you want to come in for some coffee. We could dig out the pie my mom sent home, put a little ice cream on it and share."

"That's not a good idea."

"No?" His smile was slow and lazy, his thumb resting on her pulse.

Could he feel the way it raced?

"I need to go in."

"You can't run forever, Lacey. You know that, right?"

"I'm not running."

"Sure you are. From your past and your fears and from me."

He was right.

Lacey didn't deny it, but she wasn't going to discuss it, either. "I'll see you tomorrow, Jude."

He stared into her eyes for a moment, trying to read the secrets Lacey had held so close for so long she wasn't sure she could ever share them, then he stepped back, letting her go.

"Good night, Lacey."

She nodded, her throat too tight to speak, then closed her door and locked it, her stomach churning with anxiety. She'd come to Lynchburg because she'd thought it was what God wanted, but instead of finding a client who desperately needed someone on his side, Lacey had found Jude. Irritating, frustrating, wonderful Jude.

She scowled, pacing the downstairs, checking all the doors and windows by rote. Nothing had been easy since she'd arrived in Lynchburg. Maybe that meant Lacey had made a wrong choice, headed left when she should have gone right. Or maybe it just meant that the right things were often the hardest.

She set the food Becca had sent on the counter, then opened the bag and pulled out a plastic container of pot roast and another that contained yeasty smelling rolls. The third container held two large slices of apple pie. Lacey's stomach grumbled as the sweet smell of apples and cinnamon drifted up from the container. She made up a plate for herself, heated it in the microwave and sat at the small kitchen table to eat the food alone.

She shouldn't have minded. She'd eaten plenty of meals alone. Somehow, though, she couldn't help wishing there was someone in the house to talk to and share her worries with.

Someone?

Jude.

She frowned, stabbing at a piece of meat. "Lacey Beth Carmichael, you are not going to spend the evening mooning over your client."

Sure she wasn't.

And she wasn't going to devour every bite of the food Becca had made, either. Or snack on the candy she'd bought. Or dig into the Twinkies Jude had left on the counter.

And she wasn't going to pace around the house, bored and lonely.

"You are not bored and you are not lonely." She muttered the words as she stabbed another piece of meat and shoved it in her mouth.

There was no way she was going to spend another minute of her afternoon off thinking about Jude. She was going to enjoy her meal alone, and she was going to be happy about it.

A soft rap came from the wall beside her, and Lacey jumped, her heart in her throat as she whirled toward the sound. It came again. One long beat. Two short. One long. Not a mouse, for sure. And not an intruder. The wall was the one that connected Lacey's place to Jude's, and she could picture him on the other side, knocking on the wall and grinning, his gray eyes flashing with humor, his long legs stretched out as he sat at his kitchen table.

So maybe Lacey was alone, but not as alone as she'd been before.

She smiled, echoing Jude's pattern, then dug into the food his mother had sent, the evening settling around her as rain fell from the deep gray sky and darkness descended.

NINETEEN

Three in the morning.

Lacey didn't believe in ghosts, but as she stared out her bedroom window she could understand why other people did. With the moon sunk deep below the horizon, the darkness seemed filled with danger, every shadow shifting eerily. Rain pattered on the roof and splashed the windows, the sound mournful and lonely. Lacey was sure that if she listened carefully enough she would hear the wind moaning in the eaves.

Sleepless, she stared out the bedroom window, waiting. For what, she didn't know. The early morning had an air of expectation, as if the world were anxious for the sun to rise. Lacey was anxious, too, but for other reasons.

She felt unsettled and unsure, and she didn't like it.

She'd spent the past eleven years learning to be Lacey Carmichael the confident professional rather than Lacey Beth the scared, rebellious kid. If she allowed herself to be vulnerable again, she might become what she'd been. And when she was with Jude, she *was* vulnerable.

She sighed, forcing herself to move away from the window and the darkness beyond. There were better things she could do with a sleepless night than stand staring at nothing and worrying about everything.

She grabbed her Bible from the nightstand and walked down the stairs, determined to refocus her energy. If she couldn't sleep, she could study and pray. Maybe in the stillness and silence, she would find the peace that always seemed just out of reach.

The armchair was the perfect place to sit and read, and Lacey settled into it, eyeing the fireplace and wishing she had the courage to go outside and look for wood. She could have a cheery fire, sip a cup of tea. But there was no way she was going out in the dark. Not after everything that had happened over the past few days. She stayed put and flipped open her Bible, trying to focus on the words and praying that God would give her insight that might ease her anxiety and help her sleep.

A soft sound came from the front of the house. Something scraping against the wood. It was a discordant note against the rain's gentle melody. Surprised, Lacey flicked off the light and stood, moved to the living room window and slowly pulled back the curtains. If something was out there, she couldn't see it. Which was perfectly fine with her. She didn't want to see it. Or him. Or anything else. She wanted to pretend that what she'd heard was nothing more than the wind blowing through the porch railings.

She stepped back, started to turn away and caught a movement out of the corner of her eye. There. Just beyond the porch. A shadow moved. Low to the ground, but not an animal. It looked like a hunched-over person. There was a flash of light, a glimpse of a face. White skin. Dark hair.

Lacey stepped back, her heart pounding, her mind racing. Something crashed onto the porch and exploded, raining fire and glass and smoke so thick Lacey could smell it through the closed window.

She ran for the front door, grabbing the doorknob, feeling the hot metal beneath her hand. Smoke poured from beneath the door, choking her, and she knew there was no escape in that direction. She pivoted, running through the living room and kitchen, grabbing the phone as she went. She needed to get outside, get Jude, call for help. Pray that whoever had started the fire was long gone.

An alarm shrieked, spurring Lacey on as she yanked open the sliding glass door and raced into the icy rain. Her fingers slipped on the wet gate that separated her yard from Jude's. She fumbled with the catch and shoved it open, fear crawling up her spine, making the hair on the back of her neck stand on end. She wasn't alone. She felt it in every heartbeat, heard it in the warning that shrieked through her mind.

Danger.

"Jude!" she shouted as she ran, terror lifting her voice over the splash of rain and scream of the alarm.

"Right here." He was in front of her, grabbing her arm and pulling her toward the back of the yard before she even saw him. He was limping, but moving fast, and Lacey stumbled along beside him, her heart slamming against her ribs, her eyes straining to see in the blackness.

"There was a guy out front. I saw him. He might be out here." Her teeth chattered on the words, and Jude slid to a stop.

"You're sure?"

"Yes."

"Stay here."

"No." She grabbed his sleeve, holding tight when he started jogging away. "We need to call for help. Let someone else deal with it."

"And let him get away again? I don't think so." Jude pulled open the gate. The sharp crack of a gunshot split the night, and Jude grunted, tumbling sideways.

Lacey grabbed his waist, the stitches in her hand stretching and ripping as she tried to keep him from falling.

"Get down." He hooked his arm around her and lunged behind

the gate as another crack echoed through the darkness. Wood splintered. Rain fell. Lacey landed on wet, cold ground, her face pressed into the earth, Jude covering her with his body. Something slammed into the ground near her shoulder and she screamed.

"Don't move." Jude rolled to the side, used his feet to kick the gate shut as sirens screamed and more wood splintered.

"Where is he? Where is he?" Lacey tried to look around without lifting her head, but all she could see was thick grass and earth.

"Shh." Jude moved close, covering her with his body again. Protecting her from a lunatic with a gun.

"Is he still here?"

"I don't know," he whispered near her ear. Lacey could feel the tension in his body, the tautness of his muscles.

"We should—"

"Wait."

"He's going to walk through that gate and shoot us dead." She'd felt all-consuming terror before and had hoped never to feel it again. It was back, though, crawling up her spine, claiming her thoughts and her mind. She tried to move, wanting to get up and run.

"Let him come to us." Jude pressed her deeper into the hard ground, his lips brushing her cheek as he spoke.

"Do you have your gun?"

"Does a banker have money?"

"If he opens the gate—"

"I'll do what I have to."

"But what if—"

"Shh. Just wait."

Wait?

To be brutally murdered? To die in the icy rain in a town she'd never been to until three days ago? To die before she'd ever really lived?

No, thanks.

Lacey would rather run and take her chances.

Unfortunately, Jude wasn't budging.

She tried to move, but he was a dead weight, pressing her down. Holding her prisoner. A different kind of panic filled her, and her body shook with it.

Voices drifted from the front yard, the sound barely registering over Lacey's terror.

"Lynchburg Police. Anyone out here?"

"We're back here. Shots have been fired. The gunman is on the loose," Jude called out, but didn't move.

"Stay where you are, sir. We'll be with you in a minute."

More than a minute ticked, Lacey's heart keeping time, her body trembling, her breath coming too fast.

"It's okay." Jude eased onto his elbows, lifting his weight from Lacey. "Take a deep breath, Lace. Relax."

"Relax? Someone tried to kill us."

"It's not the first time."

"Sir? Are you out here?" The back gate opened and a light bobbed across the ground.

"Right here." Jude stood, taking Lacey's hand and pulling her to her feet, swaying a little.

Had he been hurt? Shot?

"Drop your weapon, sir." The officer's voice hardened as he trained his flashlight on the gun Jude held.

"It's my service revolver. I'm a New York City homicide detective." Jude slowly lowered his gun to the ground, then took a step away from it, something deep-black and wet sliding down his cheek.

He *had* been hurt!

"Are you okay?" Lacey moved toward him, but the officer put up a hand, gesturing for her to stay put.

"Let's just take everything slow. What happened here?"

"Someone doesn't like me very much. He'd be happy if I didn't survive to see the sunrise. I guess he figured he could set the house on fire, wait for me to run outside, and take a potshot." Jude wiped blood from his cheek and scowled.

"Looks like he was almost successful." The flashlight beam rested on Jude's face. "Paramedics are out front, but we've got to secure the scene before they get out of the truck."

"There's no rush. I'm fine. I'll be even better if you find the guy who did this."

"You two can't stay out of trouble, can you?" Officer McKnight stepped into the backyard. Dressed in civilian clothes and a baseball cap, he took in the scene, his gaze resting on Jude's temple and then cutting to Lacey. "Are you injured?"

"No."

"Then how about we go down to the station to discuss what happened here tonight? I'll come to the hospital when we're finished, Sinclair."

"There won't be any need for that. I'm not going to the hospital."

McKnight shrugged. "Suit yourself. Better get the wound bandaged up before we go, though. I don't like blood in my work area. My men have already fanned through the woods behind the house. I think it's safe enough to go back out front. Ready?"

Jude secmed eager enough, but Lacey wasn't so sure.

"Maybe we could answer your questions inside the house." Her voice shook so hard, she was surprised the words were audible.

"Not until the fire marshal gives the all clear. You'll be more comfortable at the station, anyway. Too much smoke around here right now."

"But I'm not even dressed."

"I'm sure one of our female officers will be happy to lend you some clothes."

"But—"

"You're not wimping out on me, are you, Lacey?" Jude bent close, speaking softly as he pressed his hand against her lower back and urged her out the back gate.

Yes.

"No. I just don't think it's appropriate to leave the house dressed in flannel pajamas."

"It is when they look as good on you as yours do."

"How do you know what they look like? It's pitch-black out here."

"I've got a great imagination."

"You're incorrigible." Thank goodness the darkness hid Lacey's cheeks, because she was sure they were suddenly the color of a ripe tomato.

"I'm inventive."

"What's that supposed to mean?"

"It means that you needed a distraction, and I invented one."

True. They were already around the side of the house and her legs hadn't given out yet. "I think I might need more than a distraction, right about now."

"No problem." He slid his arm around her waist, pulled her close to his side. "You've got me."

What could she possibly say to that?

Nothing, so Lacey kept silent, her eyes widening as she surveyed the house. Firefighters sprayed the still-smoldering front porch and the soot-stained vinyl siding. "It's ruined."

She didn't realize she'd spoken out loud until Jude responded. "It's damaged but not ruined. In a few weeks, it'll be like it never happened."

"Too bad I won't be here to see it." The comment slipped out, and she bit her lip to keep from saying anything else.

"You don't know that."

"Sure I do. Helping Hands will send me off on another assignment, and I'll leave this burnt-out shell of a house behind."

And Jude.

She'd leave him behind, too.

"We've got a paramedic waiting to patch you up, Sinclair. The sooner we get to answering questions about what happened tonight, the better."

"Right. How about you ask questions while I get patched up? Then we can kill two birds with one stone." Jude grimaced, his arm dropping away from Lacey.

"Then let's start with the obvious. Did either of you see anything?"

"I did." Lacey hovered near the ambulance as Jude's wound was cleaned. "I couldn't sleep and heard a sound out front. I looked out the living room window and didn't see anything at first. Then I saw a shadow moving near the front porch."

"That's it?" McKnight tapped a pen impatiently against his notepad.

"There was a flash of light and I saw his face."

"No mask?"

"No. He had dark hair and eyes. Pale skin. Clean-shaven. I couldn't tell how tall he was. He was crouched low to the ground."

"Have you seen him before?"

"No." She shivered, rubbing her hands up and down her arms.

"Would you recognize him if you saw him again?"

"I think so."

"I'm done here. Let's head to the station and see if you can pull up some suspects for Lacey to look at." Jude brushed off further help from the paramedic and climbed down from the ambulance. A white bandage covered his left temple and he was limping, but none of his pain showed on his face.

"I guess you've got some suggestions about that."

"Yeah. I guess I do." Jude grinned, a feral curve of his lips that made Lacey glad she was his friend rather than his enemy.

"Let's do it, then. You want a ride?"

"We can take my car. I just need my keys." Lacey spoke quickly. A car meant a quick escape if she needed it, and she'd much rather have Bess with her than not. Especially because she had emergency chocolate hidden in her glove compartment.

"Give me a minute, and I'll see if I can get a firefighter in your house to get them." Officer McKnight walked away, and Lacey hugged her waist, praying he'd hurry back. The sooner they got to the police station and got this nightmare over with, the happier she'd be.

"You okay?" Jude put a hand on her shoulder, squeezing gently.

"Me? You're the one that nearly got shot in the head." Just the thought of the blood running down his cheek made her shudder.

"Yeah, but I wasn't. I've cheated death twice. I guess God must have a reason for that." Jude seemed to be speaking more to himself than to Lacey, and she slipped her arm around his waist, not saying anything. Just stood with him while the cold rain fell around them.

TWENTY

Jude paced Officer McKnight's small cubicle, his head throbbing in time with his beating heart, each pulse a reminder that for the second time in just a few months, he'd been closer than he'd wanted to be to meeting his maker. If God was trying to get Jude's attention, He'd succeeded in a big way.

"Does that one look familiar?" McKnight's words drew Jude from his thoughts, and he turned his attention to the small table where Lacey sat, a pile of photocopied driver's-license pictures in front of her. Each belonged to a relative of a murderer Jude had helped put behind bars. Any one of them could have been the shooter. There was one there, though, that was different than the others. Jimmy Russell. A police officer. A good one.

Was it possible he'd gone bad?

Jimmy's son had died. Jude had known people to turn dangerous over less.

"No." Lacey placed a photo in a discard pile near her elbow and lifted another one, studying it carefully. Her damp hair clung to her neck and cheeks, falling around her pale face in dark-gold waves. The black T-shirt a female officer had lent her hugged her shoulders and left her arms bare. The scars he'd only glimpsed before were pale white lines that snaked around her wrists and forearms. In some places, they were thick and corded as if skin and sinew had been scraped away.

In his mind's eye, he could see her, handcuffed and chained, yanking against her bonds, trying desperately for freedom. The anger he'd felt when she'd told him the story bubbled up again, churning and hot. What kind of man treated a kid that way? What kind of mother allowed it?

And what kind of kid survived? Thrived?

A tough one. And resilient.

Those were qualities Lacey still possessed.

She glanced up from the next photo she was studying, meeting his eyes. She must have known he'd been looking at her scars, but she made no attempt to cover them. Just lifted her chin a notch and turned her attention back to the photo. "This isn't the guy, either."

"You're sure." McKnight rubbed the bridge of his nose and glanced at his watch. They'd been there an hour. At the rate Lacey was going through the photos, they could be there an hour longer.

"Yes. He's similar, though. Dark hair and eyes. Similar face shape."

Jude leaned in to get a better look. The guy in the photo looked gaunt and haggard, his face thin and his eyes deeply shadowed. Similar to Jimmy but more worn than Jude's old sergeant had been.

He lifted the pile, sifting through until he came to Jimmy's picture. "How about this one?"

She studied it with the same deliberate attention she had the others. "That's him."

Jude's heart jumped. "You're sure?"

"Yes. Gaunt cheeks and sunken eyes. That's what I remember most about him."

"It was dark, Lacey. You only saw him briefly." McKnight

slid the photo from her hands, frowning. He knew Lacey had just fingered a fellow police officer, and he didn't like it.

Neither did Jude.

But cop or not, Jimmy Russell would pay if he was the one trying to kill Jude.

"It might have been a brief look, but I saw him clearly. That's the guy." Lacey sat back in her seat, stretching and yawning. There were dark crescents beneath her eyes and her skin was ghostly pale. She needed to be in bed, being fed hot soup and tea. She did not need to sit for another hour in McKnight's cubicle answering the same questions over and over again.

"We're going to have to find him and bring him in for questioning, McKnight. No matter how much we dislike the idea." Jude stood. "For right now, I think Lacey has answered all the questions she can."

McKnight nodded and stood. "I'm going to send some men out to local hotels. See if Russell has checked in anywhere nearby. In the meantime, I'm going to set you two up in a safe house."

Safe house?

The idea was so ludicrous, Jude almost laughed. "You're kidding."

"Do I look like I'm kidding?" McKnight scowled and stood, crossing his arms over his chest.

"I've been a homicide cop for five years, McKnight. I don't believe in hiding from killers. I believe in hunting them down."

"Yeah? Well, I don't believe in letting people die on my watch. The way things are going, that's what's going to happen if you two don't go underground for a while."

"You know what Russell will do if I disappear? The same thing he did when I was in the hospital and had a dozen police brothers hanging around. He'll go to ground."

"Not if he doesn't know we're looking for him."

"How can he not know? I've got a buddy in New York

looking for him. You're going to have guys here looking. He's a police officer. He'll know how to find that out, and he'll know what it means. I'm not going to hide, McKnight. You may as well get that through your head."

"I can't force you, and you know it. What about her?" He pointed a thumb at Lacey.

"She needs to be in the safe house. Just make sure it's really safe."

"Hey, I'm still here." Lacey stood and stretched, the black T-shirt riding up to reveal an inch of creamy skin and what looked like a deep-purple scar. Another injury suffered at her stepfather's hands?

Jude's stomach clenched, and he gritted his teeth. There was no way he was going to let her be hurt again. "Good. Then we won't have to explain the plan to you."

"I appreciate the thought, gentlemen, but there is no way I'm going to a safe house."

"Sure you are." Even if that meant Jude carrying her there.

"Look, that guy—" she stabbed at the photo on the table "—could have killed me tonight. When the bullet grazed your head, I stood there like an idiot trying to keep you upright. All he had to do was take another shot, and I would have been dead."

"I pulled you down, Lacey. That's why he didn't shoot you."

"I don't think so. He took the first shot the second you opened the gate, and he just missed taking your head off. It was only after I stepped up beside you that his aim was off."

"He was your sergeant. How good of a shot was he?" McKnight tapped a pen against his thigh, and Jude knew he was thinking Lacey might be right.

And maybe she was.

He and Russell had gone to the shooting range a few times, and Russell was a decent marksman. "Pretty good, but that was years ago."

"I'm thinking the guy doesn't know Lacey saw him tonight. If that's the case, and he's got some kind of vendetta solely against you, I think she'll be safe enough."

"I want her in a safe house, McKnight. Tonight."

"So it's okay for you to walk around town while a crazed lunatic hunts for you, but I'm not allowed to when we both know I'm perfectly safe?" Lacey's eyes flashed emerald fire, and her chest heaved with indignation, but she wasn't going to win the argument, and the sooner she realized it, the better.

"You're going. End of discussion."

"You overbearing—"

"Much as I'm enjoying your little spat, I've had a long night, and I'm ready to go home. So here's the deal: I can't justify putting someone in a safe house if she's not in danger. Lacey, you're free to go."

"Thank you, Officer McKnight." Lacey smirked at Jude and grabbed her purse. "Now, if you two will excuse me, I'm going to get my chocolate fix."

"I still want *you* in that safe house, Sinclair."

"Forget it. I know the risks. I'm willing to take them to bring Russell in."

"Watch your back, then."

"You know it." Jude offered a quick wave and hurried after Lacey. He caught up to her a few feet from the front door.

"If you're running because you think I'm going to keep arguing about the safe house, you can relax."

She glanced over her shoulder and slowed her pace. "Relax? Our house was burned, you were nearly shot in the head and now you're planning to make yourself bait for a killer. How am I supposed to relax?" She slammed her hand against the door, shoving it open and stalking out into gray morning light.

"Better watch it, Lacey. Keep getting so upset about what happens to me, and I might think you care." He meant it as a joke, but she speared him with a look that could have made a hardened criminal run for cover.

"Of course I care. Your brother hired me to take care of you. Letting you die isn't part of the job."

"So that's the only reason the thought of someone killing me upsets you?"

"You're a human being. I wouldn't want anyone to be killed."

"Somehow I don't think that's the entire truth." He grinned, tilting her chin up with his finger and staring down into her eyes. "Come on. Admit it. You like me."

"Not as much as I like chocolate. Which—" she shifted away from his touch "—you're keeping me from."

"I guess you have a plan for getting some."

"Getting some? I've got some." She opened her car door, dug into the glove compartment and pulled out a Hershey bar. "Want one?"

"How many do you have in there?"

"Enough to keep me supplied on long road trips." She unwrapped the chocolate and bit into it, pensive and quiet, her thoughts well hidden behind a bland expression.

"Something is on your mind. What is it?"

"I need to call Helping Hands today. You're going to have to find another place to stay while the duplex is being fixed. I doubt the person you'll be staying with will need my help around the house. That means I need to move on." She took another bite of chocolate and frowned, rewrapping the bar and throwing it on the backseat of the car.

"I thought you needed a chocolate fix."

"It didn't taste as good as I thought it would." Her voice broke, and she turned away.

"You're crying." He urged her back around, pulled her into his arms.

"No, I'm not." The words were muffled against his chest,

and Jude smoothed a hand down her back, her hair velvety soft beneath his palm.

"Then what do you call it?" He leaned back so that he could see her face, traced the single tear that slid down her cheek.

"Goodbyes are always hard to say, Jude."

"So don't say them. Just because the house is damaged doesn't mean you have to get a new assignment. Your contract with Grayson was for a month. There's still plenty of time left."

"I can't stay."

"Why not?"

"Because I can't take your brother's money and not work." She took a deep, shuddering breath and smiled. "And because putting off saying goodbye will only make it hurt worse."

"Lacey—"

"What happened this morning made me realize something. I'm starting to care too much."

"If I'm supposed to be upset by that, I'm going to have to disappoint you."

"You don't understand." She hunched her shoulders and frowned.

"Why don't you explain it to me so I can?"

"For a long time, my life was really difficult. Every time I thought I couldn't be hurt anymore, I was. After…when I left Vermont, I promised myself no one would ever hurt me again."

"No one will, Lacey. Not if I can help it."

"You can't. Relationships hurt. People hurt. There's no way around it." She got in her car, started it up. "We'd better go. You've probably got a lot of phone calls to make this morning."

He knew he should let the conversation drop. There'd be time to talk about their relationship after Russell was behind bars.

But he couldn't let it go.

He'd been through a lot in the past few months. Injury, near death, a renewal of his relationship with God. All those things had brought him to a parking lot at sunrise with a woman he might very well be falling in love with.

He leaned into the car, looking deep into Lacey's eyes and seeing what he never thought he'd find.

"You're right. Relationships hurt. People hurt. But what hurts more is being so afraid to feel pain that we never feel love." He touched her cheek and closed the door, rounding the car and getting in.

Lacey didn't speak as she pulled out onto the road, and Jude didn't push her to. There'd be more time to discuss their relationship.

If he survived.

And Jude intended to.

After years spent living for himself, Jude finally understood what was important. Not independence and freedom, but love. Of God. Of family. Of a woman who would complete his life. He'd fight for that as he'd fought for life. God willing, he'd win.

TWENTY-ONE

Relationships hurt. People hurt. But what hurts more is being so afraid to feel pain that we never feel love. Jude's words echoed in Lacey's head as she turned onto the road that led to the duplex. She didn't want to hear them. Didn't want to acknowledge their truth.

But they *were* true.

She *was* afraid.

To love.

To be loved.

Up until now, it hadn't mattered. She'd cared deeply for her clients and built relationships with each of them, but she'd put nothing on the line, risked nothing. She'd known when the jobs began that they would end, and she'd been happy with that.

Jude had changed the rules.

She wanted to go back to the way she'd been before they'd met, when going from place to place and client to client had felt like God's plan for her life and she hadn't questioned the path she'd chosen a decade ago.

She wanted to, but didn't know if she could.

Jude had slipped through her defenses and she wasn't even sure how it had happened.

"The house has seen better days." Jude's dry comment pulled her from her thoughts, and she surveyed the charred house. The porch was blackened and waterlogged, some of the front siding melted. Most of the windows were still intact, but it would be a while before the place would be habitable again.

"Where will you stay until it's repaired?"

"Somewhere where Russell can find me easily. How about you? Will it take long for Helping Hands to find you another assignment?" It sounded as if he had accepted that she was leaving.

Lacey knew she should be happy about it, but she wasn't.

"A couple of days. Maybe less. They've always got plenty of work for me."

"Will you let me know where you're going?"

"Sure." She smiled brightly, parking the car and hopping out. The sooner she packed her bags and found another place to stay, the easier things would be.

"Lacey?" He limped around the car, his eyes storm-cloud gray. "This isn't over. I want you to know that."

"This?"

"Us. As soon as my business with Russell is finished, I'm coming to find you."

"Jude—"

"You don't want me to? Say the words and I'll stay away." His hands rested on her waist, his fingers warm through the T-shirt she'd borrowed. Craggy and hard, his face had seared itself into her mind and she knew she'd never forget it.

She knew what she should do, but the words she needed to say were lodged in her throat.

"I'll take that as, 'Of course I want you to find me, Jude.'" He smiled, his hands tightening on her waist and pulling her closer.

She let the moment happen, inhaled the heady masculine scent that was Jude, wrapped her arms around his waist and felt like she was home. Finally. After years of wandering, she'd walked through a door that led to the place where she belonged.

Surprised, she pulled back, gasping for breath, staring up into Jude's stormy gray eyes. "I need to go."

He nodded, his hands slipping away as he stepped back and gave her room to move and to breathe. "My mother has put some feelers out. I'll call her in a little while and see if she's got a place lined up for you to stay."

"I don't want your family to go to any trouble."

"It's no trouble. You should know that by now."

She nodded. There was no sense arguing. In a few hours, she and Bess would be on the road, leaving the house and the little garden plot behind. Leaving Jude behind. That was the safe thing to do.

But is it the right thing?

She ignored the question as she picked her way up the singed porch steps and across the waterlogged and burned porch. Her door was black with soot and fire damage, and she gave it a gentle kick, watching as it slowly opened. The floor was water-stained, and glass littered the floor where the living-room window had exploded inward. The curtains sagged list-lessly and the paint had dark, wet patches, but other than that, the interior of the house seemed undamaged.

Lacey cleaned the kitchen, quickly boxing up the things she would take with her. Candy. Soda. Twinkies. Her throat felt tight with emotions that she refused to acknowledge. If she pretended enough, she might believe that leaving Jude was no different than leaving any other client.

Go upstairs. Grab your suitcase. Pack it.

She hurried up the stairs, grabbed her suitcase from the closet in the bedroom and threw clothes inside. Her makeup, brush and lotion were sitting on the dresser, and she grabbed them and tossed them on top of the clothes. As she did, she caught a glimpse of herself in the mirror. Her skin was pallid, her hair lank. She looked like someone who'd lived through a war.

She felt like it, too.

If she weren't leaving, she'd lie down on the bed and close her eyes for a while.

The floor creaked outside the room, the sound loud against the silence. Lacey froze, her gaze on the mirror and the reflection of the open bedroom door that she could see in it. Was that a shadow moving across the opening?

"Jude?" Her heart raced as she slowly turned, watching with horror as a man stepped into the room. Tall, slightly hunched and thin, with a gaunt face and deep-set eyes. The man she'd glimpsed outside. The one in the photograph she'd seen at the police station. Only he wasn't in either of those places. He was here. In her bedroom.

She screamed. Or tried to. The man lunged and tackled her to the ground, pressing his hand hard over her mouth. "Don't do it. Don't scream. Don't fight. I don't want to hurt you. That's not why I'm here. You understand that, right?"

Lacey nodded, her heart slamming so hard in her chest she thought it might burst.

"Good. I spent a lot of years protecting people like you. Innocent people. People who didn't deserve to be hurt. But you have to understand that I'll do whatever it takes to make Sinclair pay for what he did. Justice has to be served. This is the only way to do it. You understand?"

She nodded again. Not understanding at all.

"So, here's what we're going to do. You're going to call Jude and you're going to invite him over. Make up some excuse. Once he gets here, I'll take care of the rest."

He dragged her to her feet, his hand still over her mouth, and shoved her to the stairs. She knew better than to struggle. Her stepfather had taught her everything she needed to know about dealing with dangerous men. She might not have liked the lessons, but she'd learned them well. Despite her terror, she was already thinking through her options.

Run now or wait?

Make the call or refuse?

Which was more likely to keep both Lacey and Jude alive?

Lord, please help me. Please let me know what to do.

"Listen carefully, okay?" The man jerked her backward and pressed something cold and hard into her cheek. "I've got a gun. I don't want to shoot you, but I will. Jude will pay for my son's death. Whether or not he pays with his own life or by losing someone he cares about depends on what you do right now. Got it?"

She nodded, barely daring to move for fear the gun would go off.

"When I take my hand off your mouth you're going to pick up the phone and you're going to call Jude. You scream and you can say goodbye to life." His hand dropped away from her mouth, but the gun remained pressed hard into her cheek.

"I can't call Jude. I don't have his phone number." The words rasped out, all Lacey's terror spilling into her voice. She wanted to yank away and make a run for it, but she knew better. Jimmy Russell was at the end of his rope and ready to explode. It wouldn't take much for him to pull the trigger.

"Don't lie to me." He slammed the gun into her skin, and she winced, her eyes watering from the pain.

"I'm not. I've never called him."

He mumbled a curse, yanking Lacey across the room and shoving her down into a chair. "Don't move."

He pulled out a cell phone, dialing quickly, his hard gaze on Lacey, pinning her in place. "Hey, Matt. Jim here. Yeah. I'm doing okay. It's been tough. Thanks. Listen, I've had a little too much time on my hands since I retired. Thought I might check in on Jude Sinclair. See how he's doing after his accident. You happen to have his number? Thanks. That's great." He hung up and grabbed Lacey's phone, handing it to her and rattling off the number as she dialed. His flat, brown eyes were focused on her, the gun dropping to his side.

This was it. Her moment. She could take it or she and Jude could die. Lacey whispered another silent prayer as the phone rang once. Then again.

"Hello?"

"Hey, it's me."

"Everything okay?" Jude's voice rumbled in her ear as she walked across the room and lifted the teakettle, filling it with water.

"I was thinking you might like to come over for a cup of tea."

"Tea? I thought you were packing up and heading out." She could almost see his frown, his brow furrowing in confusion.

"I am, but there's no rush."

"That's not what you were saying a few minutes ago. What's going on, Lacey?"

"I guess I'm just tired. It was a long night." She carried the now-full teakettle across the room, walking toward the stove and the gunman.

She looked into his eyes, saw death in them.

Maybe this wasn't a good idea.

Maybe she could come up with another way to save herself and Jude.

"You want to have tea, that's fine with me. I'll be there in a minute." He hung up the phone, and Lacey was out of time.

Out of options.

Please, Lord, let this work.

She swung the kettle as hard as she could, remembering another day and time, feeling the same desperation, the same need to survive. The kettle cracked against Russell's head. He fell back, the gun clattering onto the ground.

Lacey reached for it, but Russell leaped forward, slammed the palm of his hand into her chin and sent her sprawling backward. "I said I didn't want to hurt you!" he exclaimed. "I said you should do what I told you!"

The coppery taste of blood filled Lacey's mouth, and she saw stars, but staying down meant dying, so she scrambled to her feet, fighting against hands that grabbed for her and tried to pull her back.

Hands from the past.

From the present.

All mixed together, dragging her into what she'd lived through and survived. She kicked backward as she slammed her elbow into Russell's stomach.

His breath left on a loud hiss, and Lacey raced from the kitchen, yanking open the front door and running onto the porch. Her foot caught on some burnt wood. She stumbled and fell hard, the breath knocked from her lungs.

"I told you not to run. Why didn't you listen?" The roar came from behind, and she rolled, facing death head-on, watching as the he lifted his gun, knowing that the past was replaying itself.

Only this time, she wasn't going to survive.

The gun exploded, and Lacey flinched, falling backward. Expecting pain. Waiting for it and for death. Instead, Russell cursed and tumbled back, the gun flying from his hand. Blood spurted from his shoulder, sliding onto the porch, mixing with soot and water.

"Lacey! Are you okay?" Jude knelt beside her, his face hard and tight, his gaze on Russell.

"I think so."

"I've already called McKnight. Go in the house until he gets here."

"What are you planning to do?"

"Deal with a problem," he growled, standing up and gently helping her to her feet.

"You're not going to hurt him, are you?"

"It's too late to worry about that." He reached for Russell's gun, checked the safety and tucked it in his waistband.

"Jude—"

"Go inside, Lacey."

Did he really think she was going to leave him there with a man who'd tried to take his life?

"If you kill him, you'll go to jail. If you go to jail, who will take me canoeing on the lake?"

"Don't worry. We'll get that canoe trip. I just want to have a chat with my old sergeant."

"I've got nothing to say to you." Russell maneuvered to his knees, his hand over the seeping wound in his shoulder.

"You've been trying to kill me for months, and you've got nothing to say?"

"You killed my son."

"Your son died in Arizona, Jimmy. I had nothing to do with that."

"You suggested the place."

"That was years ago."

"Who cares? My son is dead." He spat the words, and Lacey half expected him to lunge for Jude.

"Your son is dead because he was a troubled kid who made poor choices."

"Don't talk about my son, Jude. You didn't know him." Russell didn't sound angry, he sounded defeated. Lacey almost felt sorry for him.

Almost.

The sound of sirens broke the silence, and Russell smiled grimly. "Looks like your backup is coming. They'll cart me off to jail and you'll be free to live your life. Ironic. Seeing as how you're the murderer and I'm just the one seeking justice."

"I'm sorry, Jimmy. If I could have done something to save your son, I would have."

"I sent him to boot camp just like you said I should. I sent my own son to die."

"You couldn't have known."

"No? I've heard the stories about kids dying at those places, but I thought I could save my son by sending him there."

"Any parent would have done the same." Jude's anger seemed to have died, but he didn't lower his gun.

"Not me. I should have known. You should have known. Someone should have saved my son." Jimmy shifted, pulled a gun from behind his back.

Lacey screamed as Jude knocked her sideways and the gun went off, the sound so loud, so final, Lacey knew she'd be hearing it forever in her dreams.

TWENTY-TWO

Move-in day.

Lacey nearly danced with excitement as she pulled the first suitcase from Bess's trunk and turned to look at the house. What had once been a simple duplex now looked like a single-family home. Her home. A beautiful one. Well worth the months she'd waited, the weeks she'd worried and wondered if she was doing the right thing. Giving up her job with Helping Hands had been the easiest part of deciding to stay in Lynchburg. Working at Green Acres Convalescent Center was more than enough to fill the void leaving the company had created. Other things had been more difficult. Like accepting that she'd finally found a place to call home, believing that she deserved the joy she felt when she was with Jude. Believing in the promises he made, the love he offered.

But she did believe in those things, trusted in them and in Jude.

A gentle spring breeze ruffled her hair, the sweet scent of new growth filling her lungs and echoing the hope that had bloomed in her heart. All around her, the world rejoiced at having survived the long, bleak winter. The joy of it shone in the emerald green lawn and the delicate yellow tulips that dotted it. It echoed in every beat of Lacey's heart, every deep breath of balmy air she took filled her until she thought she'd burst with it.

Gravel crunched beneath car tires, and Lacey waved as Morgan pulled into the driveway and got out of her car. "Well, it looks like Jude was telling the truth. They finally finished."

"It's beautiful, isn't it?" Lacey grinned as her friend stepped up beside her.

"Sure. Except it's only got one door. How are you going to get into your side of the place?" She scowled.

"That door opens into my side of the place. Jude said the architect wanted to make the house look like a Victorian farm house. Jude's entryway is around the corner."

"Hmm."

"What's that supposed to mean?"

"Nothing. Just…hmm. So, where are the men? Shouldn't they be here by now?"

"I'm sure they'll be here soon."

"Yeah. *After* we drag these suitcases into the house. I guarantee they're sitting around watching some sports game on television while we do the heavy lifting."

"I doubt Jude is. He started work with the Lakeview police department today. He's probably just running late."

"Of course you think that. You're in love and ruled by your emotions. I, on the other hand, am not." She smiled, pulling Lacey's second suitcase from the trunk of the car.

"You're a cynic, Morgan."

"I know, but I can't help myself. Come on. Let's get this stuff inside. They've done an awesome job out here. Look at that wraparound porch. It's gorgeous."

It was. Lacey could imagine sitting there in the summer and in the fall, enjoying the solitude, but not alone. Jude would be her next-door neighbor, and when he was home, they'd sit together. "I've always wanted a wraparound porch."

"And I'm sure you told your hunky cop that."

"I mentioned it, but I didn't think he'd have one put on the duplex."

"He's in love, too. Of course he'd make sure you had your wraparound porch."

"You don't have to sound so disgusted."

"Sorry." Morgan laughed, dragging the suitcase to the porch.

"No you're not."

"You're right, but disgusted or not, I'm happy for you. Now hurry up. I'm dying to see your new place."

"I hate to go in without Jude."

"Did he ask you to wait?"

"No."

"Then let's get this show on the road." Morgan stalked to the front door, waiting impatiently as Lacey unlocked it.

Inside, the foyer had been widened and the water-damaged floor replaced. Instead of two small windows, a large bow window looked out onto the porch. A soft leather couch and love seat had replaced the old furniture, and a sleek coffee table held a beautiful multicolored vase filled with pink roses.

"It's beautiful." She whispered the words, afraid if she spoke too loudly she'd wake herself up from the too-perfect dream.

"It sure is! I wouldn't mind living in a place like this."

"You love your apartment."

"True, but someone went to a lot of effort to make this beautiful. And let me tell you, your boyfriend spent three hours in my shop picking out that vase. He said it had to be just right."

"It is." Lacey's throat tightened as she leaned down and sniffed the roses.

"You're blessed. You know that, don't you?" Morgan's voice held a wistful edge that Lacey didn't miss. Morgan didn't talk about her past, but Lacey had the feeling it was as painful as hers.

"Yes."

"So don't mess this up, okay? Make it work."

"I will."

"Knock knock. Anyone here?" Honor stepped into the foyer, Martha right behind her. Since Jimmy Russell's attack and suicide, the Sinclair women had taken Lacey under their wing, offering her support and encouragement as she worked to build a life for herself in Lynchburg. Now she had a new job, new friends, a church she loved.

And she had Jude.

"Sorry we're late. Jude called ten times before we left to make sure we were coming." Martha grinned and settled onto the sofa.

"He's been bugging his parents, too. Becca is about ready to cut off his apple-pie rations." Honor dropped down next to Martha, and Lacey's heart swelled.

Her place. Her friends.

"Here he comes. Finally." Morgan gestured to the bow window, and Lacey's heart leaped as she saw Jude getting out of his car. His parents pulled in behind him, but Lacey barely noticed. She was too busy running out onto the porch, smiling so big she thought her cheeks would break. "It's beautiful, Jude."

"You've had the whole tour?"

"Just the living room and foyer."

"Then we'll see the rest together." He pulled her into his arms, kissed her deeply, all his love and passion filling the emptiness that had been part of Lacey forever. "I missed you."

"I missed you, too. I thought you'd never get here. Did you get stuck at work?"

"No, I had an errand to run."

"What kind?"

"The kind that's a surprise."

"You already gave me one. The flowers and vase are beautiful."

"Not as beautiful as you."

She blushed, and he chuckled, stealing another kiss.

"Hello! You're not alone, you know," Morgan called from the house, and Jude chuckled again.

"I guess we'd better go on that tour." His hand rested on the small of her back as they made their way into the house. Jude's family was already there. His brothers Tristan and Grayson. Martha and Honor. Morgan.

Family.

Home.

The words whispered through Lacey's mind as she followed Jude through the foyer and into the kitchen. It was double the size. The sliding glass door moved to a central position on the long back wall. Outside, the garden she'd planted months ago had bloomed, bright pink and yellow tulips lifting their heads in praise of their creator.

"The kitchen is huge. Did you make an addition?" Lacey spun around, taking in the granite counters, the white cabinets and the sunny yellow paint, her heart so full she thought it would burst.

"You could say that."

"What do you mean?" She turned to face Jude, found herself caught in his gaze, drowning in his love for her.

"We knocked out the wall between the duplexes. Made it into one house."

"Oh." The wind went out of her sails, all her excitement and joy seeping away. "I guess you needed a bigger place since you're planning on working in Lakeview instead of moving back to New York."

"I needed a bigger place, but not because of that."

"No?" Lacey's heart slowed, sped up again as Jude reached into his pocket and pulled out a jeweler's box.

"No. I'm going to need more space for my wife's things."

"Wife?"

"If she'll have me."

"She might if you ask nicely."

He laughed softly, opening the box, pulling out a simple, square-cut solitaire. "The day I met you, I knew my life was going to change. I just didn't realize how much it would for the better. The more I get to know you, the more I want to know—and when I look into your eyes, I see forever. Will you marry me, Lacey?"

"Of course." She threw herself into his arms hugging him close, so thankful for the gift God had given her. A new life. A fresh start. A chance to replace the scars with memories. Good ones.

"I guess this means I'm going to have to move her suitcases all the way back to my place." Morgan sighed heavily, and Jude smiled in her direction, not loosening his hold on Lacey.

"Lacey is going to stay here until we get married. I'm going to keep bunking at my brother's place."

"So let's make sure this marriage happens quickly." Grayson stepped into the room, smiling, his arm around his new wife.

"It will if I have anything to do with it." Jude pulled Lacey close, kissed her deeply. In front of his family. Her family. In their home. A place she'd never thought she'd have. With people she'd never have imagined she'd feel so close to.

She smiled up into Jude's eyes, glanced around the room at all the people who had become so dear to her. "How does next month sound?"

"Next month sounds perfect." He kissed her again, the sound of his brothers' and sister's laughter filling the room, drowning out the voices from the past until there was nothing left but that moment and the beautiful gift of family God had given her.

* * * * *

Dear Reader,

When I began writing Jude Sinclair's story, family was in the forefront of my mind. No matter who we are, the things we learned as children set the cornerstone of who we are today. Despite many years spent living life on his own terms, Jude has never forgotten the values he was raised with. As he struggles to come to terms with his physical limitations, he must revisit his childhood, reassess his dreams and goals and make choices about the way he will live the rest of his life. Despite knowing this, it isn't until he meets Lacey Carmichael that he begins to realize how his choices have impacted his relationships with the people who love him most. Only by realizing this can he move forward into the plans God has for his life.

I hope you enjoy Jude's story and that reading it reminds you of the things we should all value most—faith, family and friends.

I love to hear from my readers. You can visit me at: shirleemccoy.com

Or drop me a line at shirlee@shirleemccoy.com.

Many blessings,

Shirlee McCoy

QUESTIONS FOR DISCUSSION

1. Years ago, Jude made a decision to move hundreds of miles away from his family. What led him to make that choice?

2. How did leaving change his life?

3. Does he view those changes as good changes? Why or why not?

4. It is obvious that Jude loves his family, but his need for independence and his desire to live life on his own terms was more important to him than maintaining close ties to them. Does he still feel this way when *The Defender's Duty* begins?

5. What are Jude's first impressions of Lacey?

6. How accurate are those impressions?

7. It is easy to judge others based on first impressions, but the Bible makes it clear that what we see is not necessarily the entire picture of who a person is. Can you think of a time when you've made quick judgments of a person based on a first meeting but have later had to reassess your ideas?

8. The underlying theme in this book revolves around the past and the way it shapes us. Lacey and Jude had very different childhoods. How do those differences make it difficult for them to trust each other?

9. The road has never been easy for Lacey. Her life has been filled with trials. How does she maintain a tender spirit and positive attitude despite what she's been through?

10. Lacey has left the ugliness of her past behind, but it is still part of who she is. How did her childhood shape her?

11. Adversity can make us bitter or it can make us stronger. Lacey has chosen to become stronger because of it. She clings to her faith, but she has a much more difficult time clinging to others. How does this impact her relationship with Jude?

12. It is human nature to want to forget things that hurt us, but forgetting doesn't always mean moving on. What does the Bible teach about living life after we've been hurt?

13. Has Lacey truly forgiven those who have hurt her?

14. In Isaiah 43, God calls Israel to forget the past and to focus on what He is doing in the present. What things in your past do you think God is exhorting you to let go of? How will doing that allow you to move forward into what God has planned for you now?

When her neighbor proposes a "practical" marriage, romantic Rene Mitchell throws the ring in his face. Fleeing Texas for Montana, Rene rides with trucker Clay Preston—and rescues an expectant mother stranded in a snowstorm. Clay doesn't believe in romance, but can Rene change his mind?

Turn the page for a sneak preview of
"A Dry Creek Wedding"
by Janet Tronstad,
one of the heartwarming stories
about wedded bliss in the new collection
SMALL-TOWN BRIDES.
Available in June 2009 from Love Inspired®.

"Never let your man go off by himself in a snow storm," Mandy said. The inside of the truck's cab was dark except for a small light on the ceiling. "I should have stopped my Davy."

"I doubt you could have," Rene said as she opened her left arm to hug the young woman. "Not if he thought you needed help. Here, put your head on me. You may as well stretch out as much as you can until Clay gets back."

Mandy put her head on Rene's shoulder. "He's going to marry you some day, you know."

"Who?" Rene adjusted the blankets as Mandy stretched out her legs.

"A rodeo man would make a good husband," Mandy muttered as she turned slightly and arched her back.

"Clay? He doesn't even believe in love."

Well, that got Mandy's attention, Rene thought, as the younger woman looked up at her and frowned. "Really?"

Rene nodded.

"Well, you have to have love," Mandy said firmly. "Even my Davy says he loves me. It's important."

"I know." Rene wondered how her life had ever gotten so turned around. A few days ago she thought Trace was her destiny and now she was kissing a man who would rather order up a wife from some catalogue than actually fall in love. She'd felt the kiss he'd given her more deeply than she should, too. Which meant she needed to get back on track.

"I'm going to make a list," Rene said. "Of all the things I need in a husband. That's how I'll know when I find the right one."

Mandy drew in her breath. "I can help. For you, not for me. I want my Davy."

Rene looked out the side window and saw that the light was coming back to the truck. She motioned for Mandy to sit up again. She doubted Clay had found Mandy's boyfriend. She'd have to keep the young woman distracted for a little bit longer.

Clay took his hat off before he opened the door to his truck. Then he brushed his coat before climbing inside. He didn't want to scatter snow all over the women.

"Did you see him?" Mandy asked quietly from the middle of the seat.

Clay shook his head. "I'll need to come back."

"But—" Mandy protested until another pain caught her and she drew in her breath.

"It won't take long to get you to Dry Creek," Clay said as he started his truck. "Then I can come back and look some more."

Clay didn't like leaving the man out there any more than Mandy did, but it could take hours to find him, and the sooner they got Mandy comfortable and relaxed, the sooner those labor pains of hers would go away.

"I feel a lot better," Mandy said. "If you'd just go back and look some more, I'll be fine."

Clay looked at the young woman as she bit her bottom lip. Mandy was in obvious pain regardless of what she said. "You're not fine, and there's no use pretending."

Mandy gasped, half in indignation this time.

Those pains worried him, but he assumed she must know the difference between the ones she was having and ones that signaled the baby was coming. Women went to class for that kind of thing these days. She probably just needed to lie down somewhere and put her feet up.

"He's right," Rene said as she put her hand on Mandy's stomach. "Davy wouldn't want you out here. He'll tell you that when we find him. And think of the baby."

Mandy turned to look at Rene and then looked back at Clay.

"You promise you'll come back?" Mandy asked. "Right away?"

"You have my word," Clay said as he started to back up the truck.

"That should be on your list," Mandy said as she looked up at Rene. "Number one—he needs to keep his word."

Clay wondered if the two women were still talking about the baby Mandy was having. It seemed a bit premature to worry about the little guy's character, but he was glad to see that the young woman had something to occupy her mind. Maybe she had plans for her baby to grow up to be president or something.

"I don't know," Rene muttered. "We can talk about it later."

"We've got some time," Clay said. "It'll take us fifteen minutes at least to get to Dry Creek. You may as well make your list."

Mandy shifted on the seat again. "So, you think trust is important in a husband?"

"A *husband?*" Clay almost missed the turn. "You're making a list for a husband?"

"Well, not for me," Mandy said patiently. "It's Rene's list, of course."

Clay grunted. Of course.

"He should be handsome, too," Mandy added as she stretched. "But maybe not smooth, if you know what I mean. Rugged, like a man, but nice."

Clay could feel Mandy's eyes on him.

"I don't really think I need a list," Rene said so low Clay could barely hear her.

Clay didn't know why he was so annoyed that Rene was making a list. "Just don't put Trace's name on that thing."

"I'm not going to put anyone's name on it," Rene said as she sat up straighter. "And you're the one who doesn't think people should just fall in love. I'd think you would *like* a list."

Clay had to admit she had a point. He should be in favor of a list like that; it eliminated feelings. It must be all this stress that was making him short-tempered. "If you're going to have a list, you may as well make the guy rich."

That should show he was able to join into the spirit of the thing.

"There's no need to ridicule—" Rene began.

"A good job does help," Mandy interrupted solemnly. "Especially when you start having babies. I'm hoping the job in Idaho pays well. We need a lot of things to set up our home."

"You should make a list of what you need for your house," Clay said encouragingly. Maybe the women would talk about clocks and chairs instead of husbands. He'd seen enough of life to know there were no fairy-tale endings. Not in his life.

* * * * *

Will spirited Rene Mitchell change
trucker Clay Preston's mind about love?
Find out in
SMALL-TOWN BRIDES,
the heartwarming anthology from
beloved authors Janet Tronstad and Debra Clopton.
Available in June 2009 from Love Inspired®

REQUEST YOUR FREE BOOKS!

2 FREE RIVETING INSPIRATIONAL NOVELS
PLUS 2 FREE MYSTERY GIFTS

Love Inspired®
SUSPENSE

YES! Please send me 2 FREE Love Inspired® Suspense novels and my 2 FREE mystery gifts (gifts are worth about $10). After receiving them, if I don't wish to receive any more books, I can return the shipping statement marked "cancel". If I don't cancel, I will receive 4 brand-new novels every month and be billed just $4.24 per book in the U.S. or $4.74 per book in Canada, plus 25¢ shipping and handling per book and applicable taxes, if any*. That's a savings of over 20% off the cover price! I understand that accepting the 2 free books and gifts places me under no obligation to buy anything. I can always return a shipment and cancel at any time. Even if I never buy another book, the two free books and gifts are mine to keep forever.

123 IDN ERXX   323 IDN ERXM

Name	(PLEASE PRINT)	
Address		Apt. #
City	State/Prov.	Zip/Postal Code

Signature (if under 18, a parent or guardian must sign)

Order online at www.LoveInspiredSuspense.com

Or mail to Steeple Hill Reader Service:

IN U.S.A.: P.O. Box 1867, Buffalo, NY 14240-1867
IN CANADA: P.O. Box 609, Fort Erie, Ontario L2A 5X3

Not valid to current subscribers of Love Inspired Suspense books.

Want to try two free books from another series?
Call 1-800-873-8635 or visit www.morefreebooks.com

* Terms and prices subject to change without notice. N.Y. residents add applicable sales tax. Canadian residents will be charged applicable provincial taxes and GST. Offer not valid in Quebec. This offer is limited to one order per household. All orders subject to approval. Credit or debit balances in a customer's account(s) may be offset by any other outstanding balance owed by or to the customer. Please allow 4 to 6 weeks for delivery. Offer available while quantities last.

Your Privacy: Steeple Hill Books is committed to protecting your privacy. Our Privacy Policy is available online at www.SteepleHill.com or upon request from the Reader Service. From time to time we make our lists of customers available to reputable third parties who may have a product or service of interest to you. If you would prefer we not share your name and address, please check here. ☐

LISUS08R

Love Inspired
SUSPENSE

TITLES AVAILABLE NEXT MONTH
On sale June 9, 2009

NO ALIBI by Valerie Hansen
Jury duty was just another chore for Julie Ann Jones—until the life at stake became her own. A series of "accidents" target the jurors, and while fellow juror Smith Burnett gives Julie Ann the courage to carry on, both Julie Ann and Smith may pay the ultimate price for justice.

HER LAST CHANCE by Terri Reed
Without a Trace
Missing mother—and suspected murderer—Leah Farley is found, but with no recollection of her past. If she can't reclaim her memories, even bounty hunter Roman Black won't be able to protect her from the *real* killer, who wants to keep Leah's lost secrets buried forever.

SCENT OF MURDER by Virginia Smith
Caitlin Saylor is dazzled when she meets Chase Hollister. The candle factory owner is handsome, charming and very interested in Caitlin. But when a special gift leaves Caitlin in danger, protecting her could cost Chase his business, his reputation—or maybe his life.

BLACKMAIL by Robin Caroll
When oil rigs are sabotaged, PR representative Sadie Thompson is put on the case. Then someone threatens Sadie and Caleb, her half-brother, to make the evidence disappear. Caleb's parole officer, Jon Garrison, is watching them both closely, waiting for one of them to slip up. He doesn't trust Sadie—can she trust him? She needs Jon's help, and has nowhere else to turn.

LISCNMBPA0509